# Fisher

## PRINCE OF TIGERS BOOK 3

# KATHI S. BARTON

## World Castle Publishing, LLC

Pensacola, Florida
Copyright © Kathi S. Barton 2020
Paperback ISBN: 9781953271082
eBook ISBN: 9781953271099
First Edition World Castle Publishing, LLC, August 24, 2020
http://www.worldcastlepublishing.com

### Licensing Notes

Cover: Karen Fuller
Editor: Maxine Bringenberg

# Chapter 1

"Ms. James, I'm so sorry, but we're going to have to proceed. Have you heard from your family?" Smiling at the funeral director, she told him she'd not. "What would you like us to do?"

"Let's start. I should have known they would not be on time." Standing up to tell her mom goodbye once more, she turned to sit back down as Mr. Edwards was closing the casket. The noise from the back had her temper flare. "I told you to be here yesterday, Louis."

"We're here now, so shut up. Is he closing the casket already?" Piper told her brother that the service was over. Her sister Mary came in, making enough noise to wake the dead. "She is having him close up Mom's casket before we even arrived."

"Piper, why do you persist in pissing me off all the time? I don't know why you were in charge of the arrangements anyway. As the oldest, I should have been the one to have done this." Mary huffed all the way to the casket. "You didn't have them dye her hair? Christ, she looks terrible."

"Because she was old and sick and died. I didn't make the arrangements, Mom did. If you have a problem with it, then I suggest taking it up with her." Piper smiled. "Oh, that's right. You didn't know her plans because when she called to tell you both what she'd done, you were too busy to speak to her."

Piper sat down with her niece and nephew while her brother and sister went to the casket. Mr. Edwards wasn't at all happy with the two of them. Neither was she. But soon, the funeral would be over, and she'd not have to deal with them anymore.

They weren't bad people. It wasn't as if they were terrible to her. They were just indifferent to anyone or anything that didn't involve them, always wanting people to cater to them — in everything. Today was no different. When they sat in the front row, she stayed where she was. She much preferred the company of their children than her brother and sister any day.

The eulogy was up to her according to what her mom had requested. When she was asked to say something about her mom, Mary pushed her out of the way and stood by the podium. When she started speaking, telling the few of them how much her mother had meant to her, Piper just let her. Instead of paying attention to her, Piper thought of the last conversation she'd had with her mom.

"You know they're going to demand you sell the house

for the estate, don't you?" Mom had been in the hospital then, her last time there as it turned out. The cancer was taking her. "Don't let them bully you, Piper. You're not that shy child you were when your pop died."

"No, I'm not. But it's doubtful they'll ever see me as an adult no matter how old I am." Mom laughed. "As for the house? Well, they'll figure that out when the will is read, I suppose. I don't have to explain anything to them. Nor do you."

"I'm ready to die, baby girl. I'm tired of fighting this war. But you gave me the best ten years an old woman like me could ask for. The camping trips. The vacations we took. You surely made this as good as I could have ever hoped for." Piper told her she'd had just as much fun. "You're going to take off as soon as the will is read, aren't you? Don't sit around being a sad mushroom about me dying. I'll surely come back to haunt you if you do."

"I made you a promise, and I will keep it." Mom nodded and closed her eyes. Piper knew what it was costing her mom to speak to her. "Mom, I'm ready when you are. I don't want you to die, but you sticking around here talking to me is costing you more than you have, I think. We've had all the fun we could, and now it's time for you to go tell Pop what you've been up to with me."

Mom nodded but didn't open her eyes. The monitor measuring her heartbeat was slowing. As per her mom's request, nothing would be done to try and bring her back. Piper let her tears flow unheeded. Her mom was dying, and it hurt her own heart with every pause of her mom's.

"Piper? Did you hear me?" Piper looked at her brother, jerked from her thoughts about mom. "For the love of Christ. Are you on drugs again? This isn't the time for you to be stoned out of—"

"I've never taken so much as an aspirin. Why would you even say that to me?" Standing up, Piper straightened up her dress and made her way to the podium. "Mom asked me to read this today. When the doctor told us there wasn't much time left, she wrote her own eulogy. Mom got sassy in her later years, so laugh if you wish. But don't be offended, please."

Looking at her mom's handwriting made her smile. She'd had the most beautiful script Piper had ever seen. Knowing she'd treasure this letter, Piper had made copies of it to read from today, and in case the others wanted a copy. Which Piper doubted.

"If Piper is doing her job and not grieving over me, I'm fucking dead." She looked up when Louis asked her to not curse. "I'm going to read just what she wrote. Word for word. Deal with it." She looked back at the writing, needing a moment until the tears dried up a little. "I've lived a great life. But now I'm going to be worm meat. I don't care. I'm more excited for this phase of my life anyway. To get to see my only love and tell him of all the adventures I've had with Piper. In my final years, we did so much together. Things that would wear me out, but it was so well worth it. Every fucking minute."

"Wait just a minute. Wait right there. What does she mean, adventures with you? We had adventures." Piper didn't comment to her sister. Her mom knew they'd not let it go on how much time she and Piper had together. "We did lunch all the time when we were in town. Remember those times, Louis?"

Peter, Mary's son, cleared his throat and stood up. "What are you talking about? Didn't you just say on the way here that you'd not been here in ten years? That you'd not even recognize Grandma or Piper if they were in a lineup? I think you said you'd not been here since Grandpop died." Piper could have hugged Peter, Mary's oldest. "Go on, Aunt Piper. Read her note to us and give us a good laugh."

"Thank you, Peter." She looked down at the letter again. "Let me see. The camping trips made me laugh so much. Figuring it all out took ten years off my life. However, Piper's driving put it right back on me. I'm sorry we couldn't do more towards the end there, but you of all people know why we couldn't."

Mom talked about the camper being renovated and how much nicer it was to be able to make coffee and brush her teeth at the same time. The Christmases they had at the shelter. Piper looked up when she got to the part about the house being sold to her.

"You took her house from me?" Folding up the letter and putting it away, Piper ignored her sister in favor of telling Mr. Edwards it was time to go. It didn't matter really what the rest of the letter said. They'd only hear what they wanted anyway. "What did she mean, she sold the house to you? You know it's going to be mine. I'm the oldest."

"You were notified of the sale nine years ago, Mary. Both you and Louis were. Not that I have to explain anything to you, but she sold it to me first, so I'd be able to use it as collateral to finish my education." Mary asked her why she thought the house should have been hers. "I've spent the last fifteen years of my life, more than half of it, caring for first Pop, then Mom, while the two of you went on with whatever you wanted to do. Without one hour of help from you two. All your promises of coming here to give me some time of my own. All the money you said you'd send, which again you never sent. She sold the house to me when it was obvious neither of you were going to come to help her. Then when it got to the point where neither of us could afford it, I sold it to use the money for other things."

"That's not fair at all. We had lives. Families to care for. You don't know how difficult it was for us to find servants to help us. And don't get me started on nannies and the like. You just don't know what it's like, Piper. Mom should never have singled you out in that letter, either. She did that to be mean." Piper moved past her brother to the front doors of the chapel. "Piper, this isn't finished. You're not going to rip us off now that my parents are both gone."

Piper made her way to the limo that had been hired to take her to the cemetery. She wasn't surprised at all when

Mary got in with her son, then Louis did the same with his daughter, Rachel. When it was obvious there wasn't enough room, Peter and Rachel said they'd take the cars. That, of course, pissed Mary and Louis off, that she'd not made better arrangements.

The graveside service was beautiful. She and Mom had picked out the marker that Mom would share with Pop when she'd been making the arrangements. It was a testimony of their love for each other, with a carved picture of them on their wedding day under their names. Mom had made sure it was also covered with the stickers of each camping spot they'd gone to, so she'd be able to remember them when she told Pop about them. Of course, Mary and Louis thought it was tacky and demanded they be removed.

"You touch even one of them, and I'll have you arrested, Louis. That is what Mom wanted, and that is what she gets." He asked her when she'd gotten so touchy about things. "The day my mom passed away with her other children too busy to make their way to be with her."

The service was quick. They were headed to their cars within minutes afterwards. Piper had brought her car here yesterday so that she could leave when she wanted too. The limo was gone, with her sister and brother arguing about how they wanted to be alone when she sat on the ground to watch the deep hole being filled in.

Piper told both her parents that she loved them and would think of them often. "I'm leaving tomorrow morning.

Or tonight if Mary or Louis stick around too long." Piper thought about talking about the letter Mom had written. She knew that Mom had known what the reactions would be. It was why she'd written it, after all. "Give Pop a hug for me. Pop, I love you so much. Take care of Mom."

The drive back to the funeral home was her time to grieve. Being strong for her mom had been difficult. But the ride gave her a much-needed outlet. She'd not get much of quiet time once she arrived to take care of the last few things at the funeral home. Getting out of the car, she made her way inside just in time to hear Louis arguing with Mr. Edwards. Putting her fingers in her mouth, she whistled loud and long. Everyone turned to her, and she smiled.

"While I have an idea what this is about, you will not harass Mr. Edwards about it. He's just the person who was nice enough to allow Mom and I to make payments on the billing until some money came in." Louis asked her for the bill. "For what?"

"The bill to this second rate funeral. Mary and I are going to pay for it. As soon as we have the billing turned over to us." Mr. Edwards moved away while she waited on Louis to continue. "We've decided to take the burden off you on this. This way, you can pay us back from the proceeds from when you sold the house. I don't think you should have gotten a thing from the estate of either of them. It's not like you paid rent or had any other bills while you were living the life of a freeloader with first

Dad, then Mom. We've decided we'll split the money five ways. You'll get one fifth, and as we're married and you're not, it's only fair that we get a portion for our spouses, as we have to support them as well. It's the least we can do for you."

"Yes, I'm sure this is the least you can do. However, the house was sold too long ago for you to be coming back on me to get anything from it. There were bills that we had that had to be covered." Louis asked her what she was talking about. "I sold the house and the contents several years ago when the bills were too much for Mom to handle after Pop died. You do know she had cancer, don't you? I mean, that was what eventually killed her. Then, just before she died, the doctor explained that this was the end and that the hospital would be a good place for her to be comfortable. So that's where she was when she passed."

"You had no right to do that. None at all." She said that since she owned the house, she could do what she wanted. "We'll just see about that."

When he walked away, Piper found Mr. Edwards. Apologizing to the man for her family, he smiled at her. When he told her he'd not worry about it if she didn't, Piper assured him that she wouldn't.

The two of them finished up the paperwork, then made arrangements for the flowers. They were going to be donated to the local nursing homes. There were quite a few of them from her clients, so it didn't bother her that she was able to make the decision about them. Most had sent small arrangements and donated to the charity that Mom had helped when they'd been able to donate.

"The donations were ample, Ms. James, well over ten thousand dollars. The children at the hospital will have nice things for their stay now." Mom had wanted to have readers with games on them for the kids in the cancer ward. "I've made sure the attorney for the estate is aware of it."

"Thank you. Mom would have been incredibly pleased." Signing off on the bill that had been paid over the years, Piper stood up to leave. "I'm not sure what happens next with my sister and brother, but don't hesitate to call the police if they become too much of a nuisance to you."

"They don't bother me. It's you I worry about. You aren't sticking around for the reading of the will, are you?" She told him she had what Mom had given her. "Well, child, you have—"

The knock at the door had her turning toward it. The officer standing there seemed as confused as she felt. He told her he was sorry about this. Rocky and her had dated a couple of times before he'd found and married Janine.

"The man out there said you had stolen from him. He said you took his inheritance. Then that woman—please tell me she's not really your sister—said the same thing." She told him, sadly, that they were both related to her. "I'm sorry, Piper, I'm gonna have to take you in until in the morning. Judge Parkerson is having a look at all the paperwork you gave to Mr. Jackson. I guess you figured this would happen."

"I did. I had hoped it would be after I left town." She put out her wrists to be cuffed, and he told her to just go with him. "They want the works, Rocky. Also, for me to be humiliated. You'd better cuff me up. Otherwise, they'll say you didn't do your job."

She was walked past her family. Peter was pissed at his dad, and his cousin Rachel walked away when she saw what was happening. Piper would bet there was going to be trouble tonight. Winking at Peter, she got in the back of the cruiser.

~*~

Judge Homer Parkerson looked at the paperwork, and his heart broke once again for Mrs. James and Piper. Up until Piper had gotten out of college, they'd been living in a very tight way. Little Piper had started working from home, and just like that, things started turning around. Then Mrs. James had been diagnosed with cancer. It was all over her body by the time they'd found it.

"Need some help?" Homer looked at his wife of forty-four years, Penny, who was sitting at the dining room table with him. "I'm assuming this has to do with that hullabaloo at the funeral home today."

"It does. The brother and sister of Piper had her arrested, telling the police she took their inheritance. What a crock of shit, pardon my language. But where were they when the two of them, one being their mother, had to decide whether to buy food or make a house payment?

Why, if I had my way, I'd make a list of every bill Piper and her mother paid, including the funerals of both of their parents, and have them pay her back."

"Why don't you?" Homer asked her what she meant. "Add up all the cost the two of them had to pay, and then divide it by the three of them. I'm sure Piper could use the money. Even selling off their home didn't pay off as much as they had hoped. Mary Margaret told me if it hadn't been for Piper having a good job, they might well have been homeless."

They both worked most of the night. Homer was sure that had Piper not kept meticulous records all along, they'd never have gotten it figured out in time. As it was, he'd gone up to take a nap when Penny made copies of it. There had been more red than black balances. Even with the total income from Piper's job, they'd still end up in the red at the end of the month, mostly because of hospital stays and medication for Mary Margaret. Piper paid every bill incurred by her mom without any complaints. Nor had she ever left her mom to deal with things herself, as Louis and Mary had done.

He was looking forward to this, perhaps a little more than he should have. But he'd liked Mary Margaret, and thought of Piper as one of his girls. He thought Piper would have been a better daughter than the three he had. Closing his eyes, working hard at making his body relax, Homer finally gave up and went to the kitchen. Penny was there waiting on him with scrambled eggs and bacon.

Homer called the jail at six-thirty to tell them to have Piper at the courthouse at eight. He even told them to take her by her trailer so she could clean up and get fresh clothes on. Homer felt so good about what he was about to do that he said he'd spring for breakfast for the officer and Piper.

Leaving word at the little hotel, the only working hotel in town, for the family to be at the courthouse at eight, Homer said to tell them if they were late, he'd find them in contempt and put their asses in jail. Mentally rubbing his hands together, he was as excited as he'd been in decades.

Homer had everything ready to go at seven forty-five. Piper arrived at ten till the hour. Her family showed up at eight right on the dot. Homer made a point of looking at the clock when they started bickering about the time.

"You're the ones that had Piper arrested. When I'm involved in such a thing, you can bet I'm going to make things convenient for myself instead of the fools that waste my time." He banged his gavel on his dais and told them to sit down and shut up. "Now, do the two of you have an attorney?"

"I wasn't aware that we'd need one." Homer asked them if they thought they knew what they were doing, suing their sister for the inheritance from their mom. "She took our mother's home right out from under us. Then she told us she'd already sold it. We weren't informed of any of that. Not to mention, she sold all the household items. Where does she get off doing something like that?'

Homer asked Piper if she'd notified them. "I did, Your

Honor. If you have all my receipts, you'll find where I sent them each a certified letter two weeks before I put it on the market. Also, three months prior to Mom signing the house over to me, I sent them another certified letter telling them not only why she'd done it, but also offering them the opportunity to purchase the house from her for us."

"See? She just took it from us." Homer pulled up the receipts he'd found in the file that held all the receipts. "I didn't sign for anything from her either."

"According to the receipts here in my hand, you both signed the attached receipts. The courier not only wrote on here who had scrawled their names, but also what you were wearing when you did." He looked at the two siblings. "Are you still going to tell me you didn't get notified? It also says he has a recording of the two of you if there is still any question about you not receiving it. Shall I call the company and have them bring us over the video of you?"

"That won't be necessary." Louis glared at his little sister. "This doesn't negate the fact that she took our home from us. My sister Mary and I had plans for our two fifths each of that money."

Homer asked Piper why they were thinking they got two fifths. "Their thinking is that, as they're married and I'm not, they should get a larger portion than I do." Homer burst out laughing before he could stop himself. "I'm not entirely sure about their math myself, but that's what I was told."

"I see." He didn't really, but looked at his notes and laughed a little while recalculating the totals to reflect their two-fifths. "Give me one moment here, if you please. I'm going to figure out how much things should have come to. Piper, did you also care for your dad when he fell ill? I believe you did. Didn't you, child?"

"Yes, sir. I was fourteen when he had his stroke. My sister and brother had already left home by then. I had to finish high school online, as I couldn't leave them alone. Dad was a handful on his best days. After the stroke, he was meaner than a rattlesnake." The little bit of laughter was sad coming from Piper. "Your Honor, I only asked for help from them when Dad was sick. Mom wouldn't allow me to bother them anymore when they didn't help with Dad."

"She was already living there, Your Honor. It would have been a waste of our time and money to have a nursemaid come in our home when she was already there. Don't you agree?" Homer told Mary he did not agree. "Well, it's too late now. They're both dead and gone, so it's nothing we can worry about now. We just want our share of what she got."

"Oh, but there is something you can worry about, young lady. I'm going to give you a running total of where the money went from Piper working, the social security that your parents received, as well as the sale of the house." He had his deputy hand the three of them what he and his wife had come up with last night. "Now, let me go over these numbers for the three of you."

Homer had all the income written on the first page he'd given them. At first look, it seemed that there should have been more than enough money for a small family to live on. Piper did make good money. There was also the addition of the sale of not just the home, but the sale of the family car and the furniture that had filled the home. The car that the two of them, Piper and Mary Margaret, had depended on was forty years old and ran like it. He was glad to know that at some point, Piper had purchased a truck and paid it off to pull the camper they'd been living in for the last several years. Homer put the old car in the assets column as valued at twenty-five dollars. He was probably padding it too much, but in the end, it wouldn't matter.

"You see right here, Your Honor? She no more needed to sell the house than she did the furniture. She is going to owe us a great deal more than I thought." Homer told Louis to hold his water. "Hey, I don't mind at all now that I know she's going to have to pay us more than we thought. This is so worth the extra night in the hotel for her bullshit. Hell, I won't even charge her for what that cost us now."

Almost giddy now, Homer had the debt part given to them. Once they were looking at it, he started telling them the numbers he'd come up with. He'd made a call last night to find the going rate for full-time live-in care for someone. He knew that Piper would never have calculated that as something to charge her family for, but damn it, they'd started this.

"Now, the way I see it, this young lady here is entitled to reimbursement for her time, as well as the nursemaid service she did for the two of you. And since you've decided you wish for two fifths of the estate...." He laughed at their expressions. "The way I have it figured out, you—you and your spouses, I mean—owe Piper nearly a hundred thousand each. Now we can take care of that here, or I can put you in a cell until such time you can pay—"

"What the hell are you talking about? I am not paying her shit." Homer told Mary to watch her mouth. "You old fool. She's supposed to be paying us, not the other way around. It's her that stole our mother's house and sold it."

"Yes, she sold it because there was no other choice but to do so. It was that or your mother wouldn't have lived as long as she did. Part of that money paid for her to have the medicine to help her day to day. The money from the sale paid for her to have treatments when it was needed." He looked at Piper, realizing he'd hurt her in doing this. "I'm sorry it's come to this, child. I truly am."

"I did the best I could under the circumstances. Mom and I had each other. I was able to be at her side when she took her last breath. We got to laugh and cry. If I had to do it all over again the same way, I'd do it. Simply because I was there when she needed me." Homer hurt because Piper was sobbing now. "She was my world and I hers. We had to do what we needed and never let it take us apart."

"What would you like to do about the rest, honey?"

She said that if the other two wanted to pay her, she'd not take it. It would be too little too late. Homer looked at the other two. "What do you have to say for yourself? I think you should be ashamed of yourself for the way you've treated your sister.

"Nothing. She's lucky she lives here in this little town, or we'd be the ones in the right." Telling Rocky to get Piper out of here, he was happy that she hugged her niece and nephew before leaving. "So, she gets off scot-free, does she?"

Homer dismissed the case and left the two idiots there to figure out their own crap. Once in his office, he sat down and shook his head. No one would believe what he'd just witnessed. He didn't much either.

# Chapter 2

Fisher didn't care so much for the way the man in the courtroom was treating his wife. But, as he was nothing more than the person that had found the body, he didn't give two shits what happened to the man after this. Murdering his longtime lover because she'd gotten knocked up — his words, not Fisher's — was still against the law.

"Mr. Prince? There's a phone call for you. I'm to tell you it's important but not life threatening." He stood up and moved toward the back of the courtroom. "It's your uncle."

That stopped him in his tracks. "I don't have a living uncle. Who did they say it was?" The bailiff told him they'd not given him a name, other than he was his uncle. "As I said, I don't have a living uncle."

Fisher reached out to his family as he made his way to the office where he could use the phone.

*I'm with Mom and Dad, and they're just fine. Dad is talking to Mom about who it might be. I know they had brothers, the two of them, but Dad thinks they're all dead by now.* He thanked Bryant. *Are you going to talk to this person?*

*Yes, but if you'd not mind keeping an open line, I might have some questions as to who this person is. I haven't any idea what it could be about.* He picked up the phone just as the others said they'd be nearby too. He was glad they weren't blowing this off. "Hello, this is Mr. Prince."

"This is Homer Parkerson. I'm sorry to have pulled you away from what you were doing, Mr. Prince, but I didn't think he was going to allow me to speak to you by just telling him I had a favor to ask of you." Fisher asked him what was going on. "I was the sitting judge on a domestic case a few weeks ago. The girl, I guess a woman, was being sued by her halfwit sister and brother. Now, I want you to know I don't usually say things like that, but they're idiots of the highest order. Anyway, they're at it again. This time it's about the insurance money that— Not that it matters, but they're after her again for things they think should be theirs. Nary a time in the last ten years have they done squat for their poor mother, leaving Piper—that's her name—there to do everything on her own. Now they want to come after the insurance money that went to paying off the rest of the bills that were incurred in caring for their mother. Bunch of losers if you ask me. Can't even find a single redeeming quality between the two of them."

"I'm not sure how you think I can help you, Judge, but

if you need me for anything, I'm willing to help." He told him what he wanted. "Do you think she's in Ohio now?"

"I don't know for certain, but she's driving this old camper that she and her mother fixed up. It's all she has in the world, you see. And a truck she purchased a while back. She works from it too, I've heard. The camper, son, not the truck." Fisher told him he understood, then asked again what he could do for him. "She was in the Smoky Mountains a few days ago. I'm not keeping tabs on her, but she sent me a postcard from there, telling me she appreciated my judgment call about her family. Sorry bunch of idiots."

Fisher laughed, then told his family what was going on. He told them too that the judge didn't seem to care for this woman's family any more than the sister did. The all clear was given, and he went back to the phone call. Asking him what he could do for him had the judge laughing.

"Well, now, I have a friend that knows you, young man. Says that you can find things no one else can. I've taken the liberty of sending you some of the paperwork she worked on while her mother was ill. It was used in the courtroom, and as the judgment was never taken care of, I still have it in the file. It's only been touched by me and her. I was hoping, from what I heard about you, that you could figure out where she is and tell her to be on the lookout for them. I don't know that they're dangerous, but with humans you just can't tell."

"What are you, if you don't mind me asking?" He told

him he was a bird of prey, a hawk. "Mr. Parkerson, I'd be happy to take care of this for you. As soon as I get the paperwork, I'll see what I can tell you about her."

"I'd need you to find her for you to tell her. I don't know if you've ever been an attorney or not, but I can't be finding her and telling her to hide out, because the case against her—those idiots again—hasn't been closed as yet. This girl, she's got nothing. Less than nothing if you want the truth of it. The camper she's been living in for the last several years is older than she is. It's a good one, I'll tell you that, and they've taken care that it's safe, but that and her job are all she's got." Fisher didn't want to run down a person for any reason, but he told the man he'd do it. "I can't thank you enough for this. She's a good girl that has been taken advantage of. She'd not see it that way, taking care of her mother and father when they were ill. But those idiots would chew a bone near gone if they thought they could make a buck or two off it."

"Why?" Judge asked him what he meant. "Why are they pursuing this? Going after their sister when it's obvious to everyone that she hasn't anything they can take from her? And why didn't they help her out with the care of her parents?"

"Couldn't tell you." He told Fisher how the father had fallen ill when Piper had been no more than a teenager. Then after he died, she stayed on to be with her mom. "Then she up and got the cancer—sad thing that. They were starting to get things paid up, and then this happened.

Piper was with her every minute too. From what I heard, at the hospital, she called her family several times to give them updates on her health. But all she ever got was their machine. Confounded people. Who does that to their own momma? Then when she passed on, they were even bitching about how the funeral should have been done up by them instead of Piper. I'd have hit them in the mouth if I'd had the chance. I still might before this is over."

"I'll find her and tell her what is going on." Judge Parkerson told him he'd pay him anything he set for it. "There isn't any worry about that, sir. I haven't been down south for a few years now. I'm thinking I might enjoy that."

When arrangements were made on how to get back in touch with the judge after finding the girl, he told him he'd leave as soon as he got the paperwork. Fisher thought about how families were so mean to one another and thanked his lucky stars he had one of the best.

As the hearing he'd been working on had been put off until next week, he made his way home to find that the paperwork had arrived already. Fisher didn't open the file until he changed out of his suit and put on something more comfortable to wear around the apartment. He had finally figured out where he was going to put his home, but he'd not thought too much about what sort of house he wanted. Probably something huge, he supposed. Even if he wanted small, the faeries would take the building he wanted and put it together, and make it larger just because they didn't understand why someone wouldn't want lots of room.

The file inside the envelope was marked with dates and names. He loved the neat print the person who had written it had. When he touched the red cover to the folder, he felt the jolt of a connection right away. It took him several seconds before he realized he was getting more than he usually did from an item.

Her face was there for him to see. She was a beautiful woman. Fisher could even see the lines of worry on her forehead, the only mar to her face. Also, she was stressed out. While it wasn't late in the evening yet, she was in the camper and laying on the bed. That was when he realized she'd been crying. Everything in him wanted to leave right this minute and find her.

Suddenly, she sat up on the bed and looked around. *Who's there?* He was worried that her family had found her. *Who's in here with me? I can feel you. Tell me who you are right now, or I'm going to shut you out.*

*My name is Fisher. Is that who you feel?* She looked around again before lying down. *Can you hear me?*

*Yes. What do you want? And how did you do this?* Fisher explained to her what he'd heard from the judge. *I heard from them today. I should have changed my cell phone number, but that costs more money than I have at the moment. They think that Mom's insurance should have been divided into five parts.*

*Do you have more family than them? The judge only mentioned a brother and sister.* She explained to him how she wasn't married, so she only got a fifth. *That's stupid.*

*Yes, well, that's them in a nutshell. Mom and I barely had* enough to live on, and they think I had it easy. *Living at home while caring for my mom should have been great for me, as I was living there rent free.* Fisher again didn't understand humans. *I'm not, you know. Not totally human. I mean, I used to be, but I got a little boost from a friend of mine. That was the only way I was able to work and take care of Mom all the time without getting ill myself.*

*Vampire?* She said that was it. *I'm sorry you had to do that. I'm sure your mother appreciated you very much. I know my mom would have.*

*She was my world. We made a lot of good memories.* Fisher told her that was a wonderful thing, memories. *So now that you've told me about them, does that mean you won't bother me again?*

*I don't know. I have sort of enjoyed talking to you. I've never been able to do this before with someone. Mostly, however, I find things that aren't anything more than a watch or some other piece of their lives. Most of the time, I'll be honest with you, I hate doing it. Lately I've been taking on the extra work because I'm bored.* She told him she'd not been bored in a very long time. *Yes, well, I've been around for a lot longer than you have. Like decades and decades longer. I'm a black tiger, the first of our kind.*

*There really are black tigers?* Fisher leaned back in his chair and told her how they'd been born the first black tigers because the queen of the earth, Lady Aroura, wanted them around to help others like them along. *What a wonderful story. I'm not sure I believe it, but it is a wonderful story.*

Fisher laughed. *Why don't you think it's a truthful story? I mean, is it that I'm a black tiger, one of the first, or is it that I know the queen of faeries?* She told him both. Fisher could already feel she was less tense than she'd been. *I was coming there to rescue you. Be your knight in shining armor. But I guess you really don't need me around now.*

*I don't know. This is the first time I've laughed in a long time. Forever, it feels like. Perhaps if you came here, we could hang out while looking at the mountains. Or have you been around so long that they were just little hills back then?* He laughed again, telling her he'd been around before there had even been a Gatlinburg. *Sure, you have. And I'm as old as the first rock that was ever seen. I'm not usually this friendly with strangers. Why don't you come down here? Nothing but friendship. I'm not in the mood to keep you at arm's link while gandering at the most beautiful mountain range I've ever seen.*

Fisher didn't have to think twice about it. Getting into his car, he started the truck up and realized he was going to drive several hours to meet a woman he didn't know in a place he wasn't sure of. He paused for just a moment to think about what he was doing.

*I don't know what came over me, Fisher. I never do anything like this. You must think I'm a weirdo. I assure you I am, but also lonely. I've never spoken to anyone like I have you. I felt something I've never felt. Compassion. Understanding. Even a little humor mixed in for shits and giggles. But I have never invited a man to come and see me. Especially one that probably lives several hundred miles away.* Fisher thought about his next move. Not to mention the words that he'd say to her. He realized then that he really wanted to meet her. *Don't do this. I'm sorry I even mentioned it.*

*I'm leaving now. I'll be there really late. Is that all right?* She asked him if he was sure. *As sure as I've been about anything in a long time. We can meet at one of those all night breakfast places that serve pancakes with pecans on them.*

*I can't afford anything like that.* Fisher told her it would be his treat. *Nor can I allow you to do that. I'll probably regret this. For all I know, you could be a mass murderer. But you can come to my camper, and I'll make us something to eat. If you still want to come.*

*I do, because I've enjoyed myself so much, just talking to you.* She laughed again, and Fisher started his truck up. *It takes about seven hours or so to get there, Piper. So, don't be upset if I show up around midnight or sometime afterwards. All right?*

*That'll be fine. I'm an early riser anyway. I have a few more jobs to do, and that'll keep me from just lying around feeling sorry for myself.* He told her not to do that. *I should have spoken to you before. You might have kept me from sitting here for three days with nothing to occupy my mind but how lonely I feel right now. I should be working.*

*We'll take it a little at a time, you and me. Perhaps we'll be good for each other.* He hoped so. Just in the few minutes he'd been talking to her, he did feel a great deal better. *Tell me a little about yourself. It will make the time go by faster if we talk to each other.*

*I'm twenty-five years old and single.*

They talked for hours. Even when he had to stop and get gas or something to eat, they spoke about everything. Keeping some of his thoughts to himself, like how easy it had been to connect with her, he also didn't tell her that he had a great deal of magic.

~*~

Piper wasn't sure she'd made a sound decision. Her heart raced each time she thought of having this stranger in her home. But after talking to him during his drive to her, Piper felt like she'd known him forever. The things they had in common, the books they'd both read and enjoyed. It was as if they'd been made for each other to be friends.

The knock at her door at midnight made her heart race. Piper wasn't sure if it was from fear or excitement. As soon as she opened the door, her disappointment was overwhelming. The officer standing there smiled at her.

"Ms. James?" She nodded at him, almost too afraid to find out what he had to say to her. "This gentleman here said he was coming to see you. I was doing my rounds here when I saw him driving slowly around the campground. He seems like a nice fellow, but that doesn't mean much nowadays."

"No, I guess not." Then she saw Fisher standing there beside the officer. "Hello, Fisher. You made good time."

"I did. Thanks for the instructions. I just forgot which campsite you were in." She nodded at him. When he smiled, Piper felt it warm her like the sun did on her walks.

He turned to the officer. "Thank you for your help, Officer. I might well have scared some campers. That was never my intention when I came here looking for Piper."

As soon as the men shook hands, Piper felt a connection with the officer. It was immediate and profound. She also knew his wife was missing, having left him several weeks ago, taking their son with her. Looking at Fisher, she wondered how she'd been able to know that.

"Officer Faraday, correct?" The man nodded at Fisher. His eyes were glazed over, his jaw slack, like he was in some sort of trance. "Your son is at the hotel on highway seventy-five going north. Exit thirty-eight in Kentucky. There is a Baymont Hotel there. He's alone but in good health. Your wife isn't there — she is dead. She overdosed in the next room with her lover."

As soon as the connection between Fisher and the officer was broken, Officer Faraday looked slightly confused but otherwise fine. He asked Fisher what had happened.

"You were just telling us about the tip you received just now. Something about your son." The officer nodded and told them how he needed to go to Kentucky to see if it was true. "Yes, that's right. Good luck. I'm sure your son is just fine."

When he left them, Fisher looked at her. His face showed concern. Instead of asking him what had just happened, she moved back so he could come into the camper with her. There was the slightest hesitation on his part, just enough that she was sure he was going to leave her now.

"I don't know what you're thinking right now. I don't even know if I want to know. But I would very much like for you to just come in and be with me. Act as if that didn't just happen to us both." Fisher said he could do that, but they would have to talk. "I understand. Just not now. All right?"

Fisher climbed the two steps and entered her home. In that moment, the second that he looked at her while standing in the doorway, she knew Fisher was going to be more to her than just a good friend. Turning her back to him, she told him where the bathroom was, as well as the couch that turned into his bed.

"I'm exhausted. I usually go to bed around ten, so being up this late is unusual for me. So, if you can find everything you need, I'm going to go to bed. Alone. We talked about that too if you'll remember. I'm not a person that—"

"Piper." Her teeth hurt when she closed her mouth. Piper knew she was overreacting, babbling too, but she didn't know what to do. "I'm not going to do anything to harm you. Nor will I take anything from you. I'm your mate, as I'm assuming you figured out. You can rest assured that nothing will happen between us until you're ready. All right?"

"Yes. But I'm confused." Fisher told her he was as well. "Bad confused or good confused? Because right now, all I can think about is touching you. Having you wrap me up in your arms and make everything better for me. But another part of me wants to turn you out and leave here before anything more happens."

Fisher smiled at her, and her already mixed up mind went into overload. Taking a step toward him, Piper put her hands on his shoulders, only then realizing how big of a man he was. As soon as he put his hands on her waist, she felt a calmness come over her that made her know she was in the best place possible.

"You're all right now?" Shaking her head, then nodding, Fisher laughed. "Yes, well, I know just how you feel. Right now, I feel as if the weight of the world has been lifted from me. I can feel that you're less stressed too. May I hold you?"

"I'd very much like that." Piper laid her head on his chest as he pulled her body flush with his. "Is us being mates why I felt the officer's pain? Also, how I was able to know what you were telling him was what he needed to know?"

"Yes, I think so. As I've never had a mate before, I can only guess. Also, I think that's why I was able to connect with you the way that I did. I have to tell you a few more things I didn't before—things you'll need to know. You're an immortal. The same as me. I'm ancient too." Piper asked him to explain when she looked up at him. "Immortal. As in living for—"

"Don't be a dick. You know that's not what I meant at all." His laughter was like a balm for her heart and soul.

"How old are you? Ancient could be a hundred years or less when you take into account that I'm only twenty-five."

"I don't think you're going to like my answer any more than you might some of the other information I have to let you in on." Glaring at him earned herself a kiss to her nose. "First of all, I have to tell you that myself and my brothers are all the same age, just different times of birth. I'm a hundred times older than you are. Give or take a decade or two."

Piper pulled back and looked at Fisher to see if he was joking or not. The look on his face told her nothing, not even when he took a step forward to hold her again. Putting her hand up, trying to judge the look on his face, it was as unreadable as if she were looking at a photo of him.

"You're serious." Fisher said he was. "I don't understand. You're over twenty-five-hundred years old? You do know you don't look a day older than me, right?"

"You'll never age from this point on, either. Nor will you get ill, gain weight, or be killed. Even if you were hurt, shot, or something equally heinous, you'll heal quickly. Like in minutes, if not too serious. Longer, of course, if it's worse. Also, you might well have heard that iron will—" Piper put her hand over his mouth. When he kissed her palm, she smacked him on the chest. "Too much?"

"You think so?" Fisher laughed again. "A person could forgive you most anything when you laugh like that. Why me? I have so much going on in my life right now that if you were smart, you'd take off at a high rate of speed and never look back. I have no money. My only possessions are this camper and my truck. The computer I use is nearly eight years old. Even if you discount the fact that I'm poorer than a church mouse, I have a brother and a sister that are out to take what little I have from me because they're greedy fucking shits."

"First of all, you're no longer broke. What I have is now yours. Secondly, you're not alone in dealing with them anymore. In one of my jobs, I was a pretty good attorney. Also — well, I had hoped I'd have a little time in introducing you to someone, but I'm afraid he's impatient." He had a child, as well as a wife, she just knew it. "Don't make up things to worry about. I have no children because I've only just met you. You are the only person I can have a child with. As for being married. I'm hoping that as soon as you're ready, we can take care of that too. Don't freak out. But there is a faerie here that will be with you at all times from now on. His name is Peter. As a favor to me, he's been keeping an eye on you since we first connected. Keeping you safe."

"Peter?" Almost as soon as she said his name, he was standing on Fisher's shoulder. "It's a tiny man. I mean, he's handsome and has wings and sparkles, but he's a very tiny little man."

"Did you hear that, Lord Fisher? She's called me a handsome little man. Why I feel as lucky about her as I am when I have myself a good nap." Piper put out her hand to touch him. Peter flew to her hand and sat down on her palm. "Why, Lady Piper, you're a very beautiful woman too. Almost as beautiful as Lady Aurora. She's my boss, you see."

"Peter, she's overwhelmed." Peter looked at Fisher, then back at her. "We don't want to scare her off on the first day, do we?"

"Nay, you'd be right about that, your lordship. You are." Peter stood up, and his wings were fluttering almost too fast for her to see. "You're going to be right fine now, miss. Those people that should be good to you? Well, they don't know who they're up against now. We'll see to you and keep you safe."

"I don't know what to think right now." Fisher sat down on the couch, and she and Peter got to know each other. "I'm assuming you're going to be my safeguard against them, right?"

"Nay. Not me. I'm only a faerie. There is an entire group of fighters that will keep you safer than you've ever been. They're ready to kill anything that comes to you without anything good in their hearts. Not right away, you see. But if they hurt you? Well, they'd best be having all their ducks in a row, I'm telling you that right now." Sitting down beside Fisher, she leaned her head on his shoulder. "Also, something else. I hope you don't mind a bit, but I've been poking into your head about some things. It's all good for you. But you sure do have a nice little plantation in your head about a home you'd like to have."

"Is that important?" She looked over at Fisher to find

him sleeping. His head was on the back of the couch, and his soft snores reminded her that he'd been up for a long time, driving. Getting up, she went to the kitchen area and sat at the table with Peter. "Why is what I have in mind for a house important to you?"

"The others, the other faeries, they've built it for you." She stared at Peter, wondering what the hell he was talking about. "We've been around for a long time, you see. And to work for such a family, the Prince family, is a treat we all were happy to have. They've been helping the lady Aurora for some time. Making sure there are other black tigers around for their magic. They need only to be there for the birth of a new cub, and one of them will be black. Just like the Princes are."

"So, they're not out to populate the world of black tigers by having sex with them." Peter assured her that wasn't the way it worked. His face was bright red too, and she had to work hard in not laughing at him when she mentioned sex. "I'm new to all of this, Peter. Will you be able to help me when I'm confused?"

"That's my job, miss. My job is to care for you when you need me and to make sure you're not harmed when Lord Fisher is away or something. He's a good man, Lord Fisher. You couldn't have done better if you were to ask me." She asked him what Fisher had meant about her not being broke anymore. "Oh, he's rich. All of them are. The lady Aurora made them the richest men around. Even when the other wives came along, bringing their goods to the family, they just used what they needed and invested the rest. You'll not have to worry about another thing concerning money for the rest of your days. Which, I guess you know, is for a very long time."

She told him about her family. "They'll try and take what Fisher has if I know them. What will happen if they win?" He told her, his voice full of authority, that they'd not get to anything she didn't want them to have. "I want them to just leave me alone. Especially now that I have Fisher here. I don't want anything to happen to him, either."

"He's a great black tiger and a man of worth, miss. He'd sooner die than to give into them people if it hurts you. And you can be certain that when they tangle with you, they're going to be taking on an entire family of the greatest tigers ever born."

They talked for a little bit more. But she was exhausted and needed to work in the morning so she could get paid. Leaving out some sugar as well as a plate with some honey on it for Peter, she made her way to her room and got into bed. It was going to be a long morning tomorrow. There were also things she needed to tell Fisher. So much good could only mean to her that the other shoe was about to drop. It was the way it usually went for her.

Tomorrow she had to call a company she'd been dealing with for the last thirty days. They weren't paying her. On top of that, they were going to sue her if she turned off their programming. For the first time in a while, Piper felt as if she could take them on and come out on top. It was a heady feeling being able to feel this good because a man and a faerie had stepped into her life at the correct time.

# Chapter 3

Benson avoided talking to the programmer company for seven days before he had no choice but to talk to her. His fucking secretary had put the call through, and he'd answered it. Because Denise had worked for his father-in-law, he'd had to keep her on until her retirement.

Miss James, owner and operator, had thought since he was part of a big company, she could make threats to him about paying the bill. Well, that hadn't worked out so well for her, now had it? She told him, literally, that she held all the cards and he'd better pay her. He knew that to be nothing more than a threat too. Telling her she had better not turn off the programming she'd installed for him, he leaned back in the chair and waited for her to tell him he could have a little more time to pay her. If he ever did. Benson didn't pay for things if he could get by with it. That was the main reason he was as rich as he was.

He'd been able to take his father-in-law's little company

and turn it into a very profitable one. Of course, he'd always thought Franklin was a sap. Giving some of the people working for him time off with pay when they needed it. Paying bills on time, even if he had a net term to pay after so many days. That had been a real money maker for the business, Not paying his bills until the smaller company simply gave up on it. He was quite proud of himself for that. His wife didn't feel the same way, but what she didn't know didn't hurt her. It was the way of the world to keep secrets from a spouse.

"You're trying my patience, Mr. Alexander. I told you when you had me write the program and then install it that there were things I would do to my program if you didn't pay on time and in full. I'm not going to allow you to take any more advantage of me." He told her he was a man with power. "Are you? So, what do you think will happen to you and your money if I were to simply turn everything off? That would include your Internet, you know. It's all hooked together. I've explained to you that there isn't any way to retrieve the information you have stored on my program. Not to mention, you signed the waiver that states that if you're late on your payment, I have full rights to take my program back."

"Are you threatening me, young lady? I'll have you know that I eat little people like you for breakfast. You're not going to do a damned thing. And you'll waive the extra fees you've been tacking onto the bill since the tenth of last month. That is if I decide to pay you at all." No comment.

He loved it when he could render people speechless when he spoke to them. "Now, here is what you're going to do. You're going to take your little ass someplace and chill out. There won't be any more of those threatening calls, nor any more messages telling me I'm in violation of our contract. I'll make your little company a laughingstock if you so much as turn one computer off. Do I make myself understood? I'm a name around the world, and people know what I say means business. You're going to have to deal with people like me all the time. Think of this as a learning experience. I'll pay you when I'm damned good and ready to."

"Are you sure about that?" He didn't like her tone and told her so. "I could care less what you're liking about me or not. You have fifteen minutes to make the payment in full, or I'm hitting the kill switch."

Benson just disconnected the call. The nerve of the little bitch, thinking she could order him around like he was a nobody. Benson didn't get to where he was today by playing by the rules, and the sooner she realized that, the better off she'd be. Big companies like his were what made the world roll around. He might even buy her out someday.

Her program was wonderful—Benson would say that about her. It did just what he wanted it to do, and he'd not had to fuss with it once since she'd put it in three months ago. When he had to have a report of sales or something other than that, he had only to press a couple of keys and there it was. Even him, as un-tech savvy as he was about computers, could make it work for him. When he'd told her what he wanted, to have computers be able to load information to a single line and be updated every time another order was taken, she'd done just what he'd been wanting. And he thought her prices were just a little low too. He would do business with her all the time, even if he never paid her a thin dime for her work.

Benson had been selling and buying since before that girl was born. To have her get lippy to him about paying would make him laugh every time he thought about it. Didn't the little bitch know he could and would own her ass if she didn't straighten up? Well, he'd won against her, and she'd better be changing her attitude, or someone was going to have to take her down a few pegs.

Benson was just putting his computer to sleep—he'd been playing solitaire all morning—when his secretary came into his office without knocking. He had disliked her since he'd been coming by to see Franklin or his wife, and she'd give him a devil of a time with one thing or another. Denise had worked for Franklin when the company had just started. So, she knew all the skeletons in his—

"I told you not to fuck with her." Denise laid the paperwork on his desk. "That is what showed up on my printer about five seconds ago. Just before it posted in big red letters to call James Programming. I'm sure you're going to hear from every one of the people you have down on the floor soon too." The paper said, several times in a row, that the system had been shut down for nonpayment of bill. "I've checked too. That is on all the computers. So, the entire company knows you're a cheap fuck, and that is why the company is coming to a stop. I so wish Franklin were still around."

Almost as if she'd let them come through, his phone started pinging that he had calls coming in from different departments. Sitting back down, he asked Denise what she was talking about. He thought she was taking too much pleasure in the fact that his company was shut down.

"Well? Start it back up again. I've seen you restart your computer when it acts up." Denise told him all the computers were shut down. There wasn't any way to turn them back on when the program that connected them all was gone. "What do you mean, it's gone? There is no way she was able to shut down my company so quickly."

"Obviously, there *is* a way, and she did it. I'd say she knew just what she was doing when she put in that kill switch for this company. It's really too bad that more companies you've treated the way you tried to treat her didn't have a kill switch." He told her to shut up. "Sure, I can do that. But there is something else you should know, Benson. The data we have been storing on her program? Well, it's all gone. I've read over the contract, and you're fucked as of the moment you decided your way was the only way things should go. By the way. I quit."

He was still sitting at his desk when he realized two things. He really was fucked, and that a little bitty company had taken him down. Picking up his phone, he pressed the number that he had for her company. It was time to get things organized and back to working order. Or, he thought, heads were going to roll.

Benson thought she damned well have better saved his data. Otherwise, he was really going to own her ass. When the phone was answered, Benson started talking before he realized it was a recording. He had to call the number back twice before he understood the message he'd gotten.

"Hello, Benson Alexander. This phone call and any other future calls are no longer going to be answered by this service. You were given a stipulation, and you chose to ignore it. You will be notified by mail of all the charges that have been added to your original bill. James Programming will no longer do business with your company nor any of the subsidiaries you own. Have a nice day."

"Have a nice day? What the fuck is that supposed to mean?" Benson turned his phone off and sat there with his head in his hands. "Jesus H. Christ, she did just what she said she was going to do. Exactly like she'd threatened."

There wasn't going to be coming back from this, not with all his data missing. He just knew he'd fucked with the wrong person. Picking up the phone again, he called his wife. She must have heard from some of his managers because she started in on him as soon as she answered. "I'm sorry, love. I truly am."

"I knew this was going to happen, Benny. I tried to tell you when I read over the contract that this person was savvy, and they'd not take you screwing around with them. Now, look. You've killed my father's company because you're a cheap bastard that thinks you know so much more than anyone else. My father would be rolling over in his grave if he knew you'd tried to screw a little company. They're what made him the man he was." He told her it wasn't completely his fault." Oh no? Then who do I have to talk to about them being fired over this? Did you tell someone to pay the bill? Did you tell her you were going to do it before she shut us off? It's gone, isn't it? My family's entire company is in ruin because you had to be the big man you're not. Fucker. I'm so mad at you right now I want to bash your head in. Don't you dare come home. If I see you, I might just follow up on handing you divorce paperwork the minute you cross over the threshold. I'm so glad I kept the house in my name. At least we have that to fall back on when the creditors come calling."

"Honey, please don't hate me for this. I forged your name to the paperwork several years ago. I used the house as collateral for the villa in France." Silence. It was the worst kind of screaming at him as far as he was concerned. "Beth? Are you there?"

"Yes, I'm here. I have no idea why I'm still here, but this is the last straw, Benny. Don't bother calling here again. Don't expect me to be there for you either. I'm finished. Forever. I told you the next time you did something stupid, I was going to divorce you. Thankfully, I had a prenup signed when we were married all those years ago. I'm done with you." The phone was still humming its song of disconnection when he put the phone back in the cradle.

Getting up, he made his way to the lower levels where his car was parked. He was glad now that he'd driven himself to work today. It seemed like years since he'd talked to Miss James. He was a ruined man. There wasn't any way he was ever going to recoup his business now. Nothing to do but to find himself a place to hide out and stay there until things settled down. However, he didn't think that was going to be anytime soon. Then there was also the fact that his wife, who owned everything they had, was pissed enough to more than likely ask for and get a divorce from him.

His cell was ringing when he got into the car. Benson didn't know the number, but he thought perhaps he should answer it. The man at the other end of the call told him his name as well as who he was working with—none of which he caught when the man paused.

"I'm sorry. I've just had something terrible happen and didn't catch all that." The man, Fisher Prince, told him he worked for the company James Programming. "Yes. All right. What is it I can do for you, sir? As I said, I've been having an issue on my end."

"I asked if you were going to pay off what you owe Miss James. The full amount plus penalties. You still have an hour before the program is completely washed out. I'm sending an itemized bill to your fax machine now." He told the man he was not in his office at the moment. "I'd like to suggest that you get your ass back up there and see what the bill is. Pay it and keep your mouth shut."

"I'm going there now." He didn't get pissy when the man told him to hurry twice more. "I'm almost there. Just tell me the amount, and I'll pay it as soon as I get to my office."

It was much higher than he thought it should have been, but there was no time to quibble about it. If he could get his data back, he knew he'd be able to keep going. Then perhaps his wife would think about not kicking him to the curb.

Paying the amount in full had him hoping he'd done it correctly. Mr. Prince, the attorney for James Programming, told him as soon as it cleared everything would be turned back on. Almost as soon as he said that, Benson's desk phone stopped pinging red lights, and his computer came back online. Sitting there, waiting on Mr. Prince to tell him what he was to do now, he nearly sobbed when Prince told him it had been restored.

"Mr. Alexander, there isn't any way you can blame this on James Programming. You were warned, several times as a matter of fact, that this could and would happen. The fact that she heard from your wife just prior to calling you is the only reason Miss James held the program for her. However, you will no longer be able to do business with this company. Not even for upgrades or for any other programs. Do you understand?" He said he did. "Good. You have a nice day, sir. James Programming is no longer going to service your company or any subsidiaries you own."

Putting the phone on the desk, Benson did something he'd not done in a very long time. Longer, he thought, than he should have let it go. He prayed, thanking the Good Lord for letting Miss James have a better heart and business sense than he did. Also, for his wife to take him back. But he had a feeling she really was finished with him. Benson would even bet he would no longer be working for the company. She'd cut him off faster than he could blink. And sadly, he deserved it.

Going to a hotel, his only option, he thought, he didn't bother calling his wife. What could he say to her that she'd not just cut down? He'd been a total fuck up since her father had died, and he'd taken over the business. There was only so much he thought anyone could take, and his wife had had more than her fair share of hardships concerning him.

Self-reflection wasn't something he'd done before, but as he sat in the hotel room, he did just that. Thinking about his wife, he realized he'd been worse than the worst kind of husband.

There had been no children of their union because he'd not wanted to share his money. Benson had never wanted his nights filled with the noise of little ones running around. Nor had he wanted to have to parade his ass around to school events or the like. Now it was much too late for him to even consider how he'd hurt Beth with his attitude.

Benson also knew he'd have to train someone to take

his job over someday. The thought of telling someone all his little tricks wasn't something he wanted to do either. It occurred to him at that moment that he'd been just what his wife had called him — a selfish prick. Benson had never felt like she'd been giving him any kind of fair assessment. But right now, he knew she'd been absolutely correct. In all things. Damn it, he thought. There was nothing he could do about it now. He'd fucked everything up by trying to be bossy to a company with more integrity than he'd ever had.

~*~

Fisher watched Piper pace. She was good at it too. While most people would walk in a straight line to and fro, she moved around the camper, touching things, putting things away while she spoke to herself. Once in a while, she'd ask him a question, but for the most part, she just talked to herself.

"How did you know he would pay if I simply turned off the Internet?" It took him a second to realize the question was being put to him. "You took a big chance with this. Don't you think?"

"No. I mean, I have an idea what could be happening with the program if you had turned it off. But in just turning off the Internet, it scared him enough that he thought he was screwed over. Why did you call his wife?" She told him. "Okay, I guess that makes sense. She is the one that would be in charge of the money if she owned most of the stock. Do you think she'll do what she said and divorce him?"

"Yes. He's done this before — several times, as a matter of fact. The fact that she didn't know about how he'd used the house as collateral really hurt her. I think that hurt her more than him fucking with her family's company." Fisher knew he'd have been hurt by that too. "You doubled the price on what he owed me. I'm not sure that was the way to go with him. It didn't take me anything at all to just turn the Internet back on."

"How many days was he late on paying you in the first place?" Piper told him he was ninety days late on a net ninety payment. "I don't think doubling what he owed you was nearly enough. While I don't know how long it takes you to write a program, I believe you're underselling yourself. But then that's just me. Will you please come here and hold me? My cat is all jumpy because you're jumpy."

She stared at him. "That's the stupidest pickup line I've ever heard." He laughed at her. "I do sort of feel like my skin is on fire for some reason. Is that the reason? Because I need you to touch me in some way?"

"Which way would you like for me to touch you?" He could hear the huskiness in his voice. The need to be with her, hold her, touch her bare skin, made his cock swell and thicken. "I'm not suggesting anything, but the thought of touching you is making me sort of stiff."

"Sort of stiff? I'm standing five feet from you, and I can see how hard you are. Why do men do that? Get all hard at any kind of thought of touching skin?" He didn't have an answer for her, so he just watched her as she moved toward him, but stayed away too. "I don't know a great deal about sex. I've sort of had it, fumbling around in the back seat of a car. Trying to figure out how a condom was put on. Things that I suppose someone my age has figured out. I didn't date too much after my dad passed away."

"I don't imagine there was a great deal of time." She sat on the floor in front of him. Not in a sexual way, but just sitting on the floor. Not that his cat cared what sort of pose she was in, he just wanted her. "I've spoken to my parents about finding you. My dad, of course, has spread it all over town that I'm here with you. Also, you've not met her as yet, but Harper, my brother Bryant's wife, has been looking into things about your family."

"Are you changing the subject? Or is it important that I know these things right now?" He told her he thought it was safer if he changed the subject. "All right. But safer for who? Never mind. What did Harper find out about them?"

"Your sister is broke. Again. I guess every four years, or so, she gets herself into a position that makes it so she can't make her house payment, nor pay anything to the private school where she sends her son. This time there doesn't seem to be a way for her to get out of it. Gambling, I was told. Peter, by the way, he's a great kid. Harper was impressed by a great many things she found out about him and your niece Rachel." Piper told him she liked the kids better than she did her brother and sister. "I can understand that. In a couple of weeks, they'll both be eighteen and have already made plans to leave the houses. Rachel had a scholarship to Brown, but she's not going to be able to take it. Louis *borrowed* against it to pay for some material to be printed up in a scam he's running. Harper is looking into that too."

"What about my sister? I know she's been in trouble before with money. When I called to tell her Mom was in the hospital, she thought I was a bill collector and screamed at me for ten minutes before I was able to let her know it was me." Fisher told her what he knew about both of them. "I don't know all that much about it, but even I can tell that selling property you don't own is against the law. And gambling has always been a problem for Mary. What happened with Louis? Did someone get wind of it?"

"Yes. Harper did it just before she told me what was going on." When Piper smiled, he grinned with her. "She has some pretty impressive contacts and dropped a few hints here and there so that it would be looked into. Will you come up here and sit with me?"

"In a minute. I need more information." Fisher thought about sitting on the floor with her, but he was sure that would scare her. She seemed to be skittish about things like that. "That's the reason they're pushing so hard to get something from Mom's estate or me. Isn't it?"

"Harper said Louis is getting to the point of desperation about money. She told me he's purchased a gun. While she doesn't have any idea what he is going to use it for, she wanted me to ask you if you'd be willing to go home with me so we can all protect you from him. If that's what his plan is." Piper asked him if he thought he was going to kill her. "He can't kill you, not with you being an immortal. But he can hurt you physically and mentally. I don't want to have to kill him for hurting you in any way."

"Does he know where I am? Before you answer that, there are things I have to tell you. I can't leave here. I mean, I could if I wanted to skip out on not paying the rental fees I owe, but as it stands right now, I owe about five hundred dollars' worth of back rental money." Fisher asked her if she'd allow him to pay it for her. "I have the money now, but in addition to the money I owe here, I also have some truck issues. It's ten years old and starting to show its age. I don't think I can make it there with what I have going on. And it'll cost me more to have it fixed than I have at the moment. Even with the money from Alexander."

"My truck is brand new and can pull the camper if you'd like to sell your truck while here. The other option you have is, if you'd allow Peter to fix things for you, the truck and the camper will be new once he knows he can fix it up for you. You're his world right now." She looked at the little man sitting on the counter in her kitchen. Peter's head was nodding so quickly it was comical. "Whatever you want to do, it's fine with me. You're my world as well."

She didn't say anything but continued to stare at Peter. When she spoke, it was soft and emotionally filled. "Mom and I went to the auction where this was being sold off. It was raining so incredibly hard that even with umbrellas, we were drenched. It was still early May. There was only one other couple there because of the weather. Anyway, I was able to get this one and a second camper for less than I would have paid for one of them on a lot." She turned and looked at him. "We decided to work on the better of the two of them. Shining the outside up so that it gleamed brightly. Getting some of the parts from this one was easy, finding other things wasn't so much. But we made that sucker look fantastic. We sold it for a lot of money, to us anyway, and used that money to fix this one up. There are so many memories here that I don't know if I can part with it."

"Then don't." They both looked at Peter when he spoke. "My lady, you can take it home with you now that the house is complete, and use it for your office for your job. It would be easy for us to make sure it was a good safe place for you to work."

"I've thought of that too." A spark of happiness lit up her face, and right then, he knew he'd make this work for her. Even if he had to carry the damned camper on his back. "You said the house was complete. While I'm not sure what you did, I'm excited to see it. I'm excited about everything, to be honest with you. Will you hold me, Fisher?"

"Forever." When she got up off the floor and sat on his lap, he saw Peter disappear. "I have a ring for you too. Aurora gave each of us a stone to use to bring our mates into the family. By the way, she is going to come and see you soon. She said she wishes to meet the woman that took my heart."

"I'd love to meet her. Someday." The tiny camper tightened a little, and Fisher looked at the beautiful woman who was suddenly there. "What was that?"

"Aurora, I'd like for you to meet my mate, Piper James Prince. Piper, this is the lady of the earth and creatures, Aurora, the queen of the earth." Piper and Aurora stared at one another for several seconds until Piper got up and stood in front of her. "I told you she was real."

The slap to the queen's face from Piper startled him to the point where he had to hold tightly to his cat. They never spoke, but Aurora looked to be holding back tears. Fisher asked what was going on just as the two of them hugged tightly.

"My mom died."

The women sobbed and talked over each other. The two of them clung to each other for something akin to support. Fisher decided to give them time, whatever they needed. While he didn't have any idea what was going on, whatever it was, he knew they needed each other in that moment.

Stepping outside, he noticed the camp manager coming toward him. Meeting him halfway, he told him he was just coming to pay the bills that Piper had. The man looked confused for a second, then nodded. In twenty minutes, not only did he have the debt paid off, but he also paid him an extra hundred dollars for being such a nice person about waiting.

Fisher sat in the chair outside the camper and waited. As he was there, the faerie that Peter had chosen for him, Snowflake, was to arrive. Things were moving along now, he knew. Slowly, but moving. He was as happy as he'd been in a long time.

# Chapter 4

Louis tried his best not to draw any attention to himself as he walked up and down the streets. How anyone could enjoy this place was beyond him. The noise was too much, but the crowds of people, all of them seemingly having no concept of personal space, were making him crazy.

He'd read about Gatlinburg for years, how it was the gateway to the Smoky Mountains. What he'd not known or anticipated was how many touristy things were on the streets. Every block, it seemed to him, was another place selling the *best of* whatever they'd been selling. There were four, he had counted so far, that touted the best fudge. There also seemed to be a great many pancake houses.

Stopping just short of walking over a woman and her fifty kids, he looked to where he'd come from. Not even a block yet, and he was ready to pull out his gun and kill them all. She really didn't have that many kids, but they sounded like that many to him. It made him happier than he'd been in a while that his daughter had been sent away to school when she was young. He'd missed all the whining and tugging on himself because he'd had the foresight to not have her around.

When he was able to move again, he made his way to the restaurant where he was to meet his sister, Mary, who had flown in yesterday. He'd driven down and wished now that he'd had the money to fly. Finding a parking space that he didn't have to pay so much for was nearly impossible. Not to mention, the crowds of people were only second to the number of cars that went up and down the strip. Christ, he hated crowds of people.

Slipping around the woman, he nearly fell off the sidewalk when a huge man bumped into him from behind. He needed to have some sort of ring around him, Louis decided. Something, anything that would keep him from having to be so close to these people.

Finally getting to the restaurant where his sister was, he sat at the table and was thrilled to find a glass of water and a Manhattan waiting for him. Mary knew him well. Drinking the water straight down, Louis was ready for his drink and some conversation. Or he hoped a resolution to the situation about their mother's estate. But first, Mary told him, they had to order. She was starved.

After finding out that Mary was going to pay for their meal, he ordered what he wanted instead of what he thought he could afford. Mary was good at keeping some money around for things like this. He'd never been as broke as he was right now. Not to mention the FBI was looking for him.

"I know she's here. I've had a man following her for the last week." Louis asked Mary if she was in a hotel. "No. Believe it or not, she's in one of those really expensive campers. Streamline or something like that. No, it's an Airstream. No doubt spending our share of Mother's money on it so she can hide from us."

Louis thought Mary was right, but he didn't comment. Sometimes Mary could be pissy about repeating what she said, even if it were only to agree with her. When his salad was set in front of him, he knew this was going to be a good place to eat. Digging in while Mary filled him in on what Piper had been up to, he only listened to about half of it.

Louis didn't hate his sister Piper. Not like Mary did. He really didn't have any feelings about her at all. She was his sister, but they never hung out together. They didn't get together when they were not busy.

Piper had been born so long after him that he didn't have a thing in common with her. Not that he thought it would have made any difference. He barely got along with Mary most of the time. Unless they were plotting or arguing, they had little in common either.

Leaving Piper to care for their dad seemed to be the best way to have handled the situation back then. Not that he did it any differently when Mom got sick. Piper was there with them, so there wasn't any reason for him or Mary to come and help her out with all the extra care they needed. And sending them money wasn't something he thought he should have to do. Louis didn't expect his children to bail him out when he needed cash. Though lately, he thought he might have to hit them up for something.

"Are you listening to me?" He said he was and repeated back the last thing he'd heard Mary say. Mostly it was always about Mom's money anyway. "All right. But if you think you can bring yourself to add to the conversation once in a while, that would be great."

"The money from the insurance should be ours like we've said all along. Christ, it's not like Piper didn't have a roof over her head and wasn't sponging off Mom the entire time she lived there. Right?" Mary said she'd even driven their old car. "See? That is her payment. Just like we've been saying all along. The fact that there are bills from the shit that was going on isn't our problem. Mom made the bills. Since she's dead, they should just simply be paid off. It's not like we want the world—just our fair share. That judge, he had it all wrong about the money we should have been paying for Piper to help our parents out. I think it should be divided five ways no matter what he comes up with."

He'd been surprised by how much it would have cost if they'd paid for someone to come in and help Piper out once in a while. To add in that she should have been paid by them to clean up was stupid too. What did the judge think would have happened to the money if they'd had it to send to her? She would have blown it all, and they'd still have bills to pay.

"I do know she's not paying for staying in the campground she's in. The man I spoke to about it says Piper is in arrears for over five hundred dollars. Makes me wonder if there is any of the insurance money left. Did she spend it all, and we're going to have to sue her for it? I hope to Christ, not. I don't want to have to wait around for it while she gets her shit together. Does she even have a job?" Louis said he'd never heard if she worked or not. "Me either. But you can bet that if she has spent all our money, she's going to get herself one. I don't want to have to wait while she gets paid every week, but if that's what it takes to teach her a lesson, then I'm all for it."

There was no way Louis could wait that long. He needed money now. The foreclosure of his home was rapidly coming around. He'd not told his wife or daughter yet either. Louis was surprised lately that every time he pulled into his driveway, there wasn't a bunch of bankers there with one of those large signs that said he was in arrears for house payments. Now he had to meet up with some guy about the scam he was running to make a little extra money through the harder months. Well, every month of late.

"I'm going to go there and have a few words with her today." Louis asked if he could go. "If you'd like. But I'm doing the talking. I want her to tell me what the fuck she's done with my mother's fifty-thousand-dollar life insurance policy. I know she had one too."

"Fifty grand? Holy shit, Mary, that'll be nice to have." She agreed with him. "I was thinking I'd take her camper for now. Just to have someplace to go for a few days. I'm under a lot of pressure."

"You got caught, didn't you?" He nodded and told her what he had waiting for him at home. "I can't bail you out, Louis. As much as I wish I could, I'm in debt too. The last few times at the tracks, I've lost big time. If my husband finds out I'm gambling again, he's going to take the house and all the other things I've come to love away. Including the nice car and spa time I have every month."

"I know. That's one of the reasons I've not asked you. I saw your husband Paddy the other day. He was talking to a buddy of his about how much he wanted to get out of the big house. I guess he figures with Peter going away to college, he'll be able to sell the house and downgrade to a simpler home." Louis knew that Mary had borrowed money against the scholarship Peter had gotten, just as he'd done with his daughter's. There wasn't any way for him to pay it back either. Not ever. "I'm guessing since he didn't mention how he'd have to pay off the mortgages first, that you'd not told him about the loan you'd taken out."

"No. And if I can get the money from Mom's insurance, that will go a long way in me trying to win back everything I owe." He asked her if she was going to gamble her part away. "You make it sound as if I'm going to lose it all.

I'm not. I've gotten smarter about a great many things, and gambling everything isn't the way to win anything. I'm hedging my bets by putting money down on a lot of different things. That way, if only a couple of them pay off, I'm still ahead of the game. I like being ahead."

"Yes, I do as well." He'd never understood the desire to gamble. Having odds and stuff like numbers wasn't anything that he ever understood. Sometimes when Mary would go on about her odds and the money she'd win if they hit, it was all like a foreign language to him. He also didn't point out to her that she rarely if ever won anything close to what she spent. Ever. "When are you going to go to see her? I don't have anything going on, but I would like to know I have a place to sleep tonight. You don't think she'll object to being put out of her camper, do you?"

"Of course, she will. That's the fun part of doing it my way." Louis nodded. Not really agreeing with her but just going along. "Once your things blow over, you and I will burn it. That'll make me feel so much better. Just knowing that piece of shit she had Mother spend money on is gone will make my entire day."

Mary picked up her cell phone when it rang, but put it back down when she saw the picture. It had gone off several times while they'd been eating. Louis knew who it was. Paddy. The ring tone that Mary had set up for her husband was a theme song to some old fifties show. Louis didn't know the name of it, but he could remember the plots of the show. Two women living together and working at the same brewery while trying to fend off two odd men that had stranger names than the show had. Now that he thought about it, Louis thought one of them was called Squib or Squishy. Something like that.

"Does he leave you a message?" She nodded, but he could see she was entirely too upset for it to be loving messages. "What does he say, Mary? Anything I can help you get out of with him?"

"No. I mean, I don't know what he's saying in them. I know he's leaving me messages, but I've not listened to any of them. I'm worried he's found out something, and I don't want to have to deal with it until I can tell him it's taken care of. That's why I need this money so badly. To not lose my marriage over this. I'm going to point that out to Piper too. Her inability to do what is right for us is costing me my marriage." Again, he didn't say anything. Louis knew for a certainty that Paddy was even pissed off at Mary before their dad had died. "After today, I'll have a nice sit down with him and show him how hard I've been working on getting things back to normal. I've been thinking about gambling too. I need to slow down and only do it a couple of times a week instead of every day. You think he'll agree to that for me?"

He didn't but assured his sister it was very good of her to cut back so much. Paddy didn't believe in gambling. Nor did he like the fact that his wife was deep into it. If he knew half the shit Louis did about his wife's gambling, he would have divorced her years ago. She'd been skimming money from his business before Mom had gotten sick. Lately, he knew she was taking a great deal more than she could ever cover. And once Paddy figured that out, he'd have her arrested and put in jail rather than send her to a gambling clinic this time.

Once the check was paid, they headed out the door. He was dismayed to see the traffic of people coming and going. Being in a quiet restaurant had given him a breather from thinking about it. Now that it was getting later in the day, the crowds seemed to have tripled. Louis hated people.

It took nearly an hour to get from the place he'd met his sister to the parking garage she was using. While he was sure she was supposed to pay for the ticket to park before she entered, Louis knew her well enough to know she'd skipped out on that. He wished he were half as savvy about shit like that as Mary was.

The campground was still another forty minutes away, she told him. Belting himself into the seat never seemed like enough when Mary was behind the wheel. She took corners too quickly, drifted off the road while talking to him, and even took out a mailbox on the way to the place. Never once did she slow either her mouth or the car. Louis wished he'd remembered that when she'd asked him if he wanted to drive. He would the next time they were out together.

It was dusk when they pulled into the parking lot to the campground. There wasn't anyone at the front office by then, having closed up at five. He supposed they were out the door before the second hand passed the twelve. He would have been if he'd had to work anywhere.

The place was nearly empty as they drove around. He'd been looking for the lot number three on his side of the car while Mary did the same on her side. By the time they'd made their way around twice, he was sure she'd had the number wrong. There didn't seem to be a single three in the entire park.

"There it is." He looked to where she was pointing and saw that not only was there no camper in the place, but there was a lone bag of trash out by one of the stones that divided the space from the road. "Where the hell is she? She was here just this morning. My spy told me she was staying put because she hadn't the money to pay the bill. What could have changed in the last few hours?"

"Maybe they had her towed." It sounded logical to him, but Mary just glared at him. "It could have happened. Or, you don't think she used more of the money that is supposed to be ours, do you? Damn it. She's spending it as if it belongs to just her. If she keeps this up, there isn't going to be enough for her to have any of it."

"What makes you think she's going to get any of it in the first place? After all she's put us through in the last few weeks, I'd say we should just cut her out altogether. I mean, she did sell off the house without giving us a part of that money." He'd not even considered that. "She should have thought of us first thing, Louis. We're the only family she has. Now she's out there someplace spending our mother's money as if she doesn't have a care in the world. I'm telling you right now, that if she's spent it all, I'm going to kill her. I'm not joking around about that either. She'll be dead."

Louis believed her. And if she didn't do it, he was going to. Just last week, he'd put a hundred-thousand-dollar policy on his sister and made himself the beneficiary. He was going to get his money one way or the other. And he really did prefer to get it legally, after she was dead.

~*~

The drive was much better this time. It was light out, which made it so he could see some of the scenery. Fisher had talked to Piper on the way down, but having her seated right next to him was so much more enjoyable. He could see her expressions as well as hear her laughter. It was well worth losing sleep on the way down just to be with her now.

"I'm so excited to see how this is going to work out for me as an office. Just knowing I can still work is such a relief, since I wasn't sure I could continue. Thank you so much for helping me sell my truck. That was much easier than I thought it would be. And I promise to pay you back every penny for the camping pay off." He didn't tell her again that what he had, she did too. It had upset her so much she'd cried. That hurt his heart way too much for him to want to do that again. "Peter said my office will be easy for them to set up. And he'd make sure there were plenty of views I could see while working. I wonder how much of a distraction that will be."

Fisher didn't need to answer her. She was rambling and didn't require anyone to comment. It was, to him, something he'd never witnessed before—a person emptying their head of all thoughts until they felt they could slow down and speak normally. He realized she was quiet. Glancing at her while he drove, he asked her if she was all right.

"I am. I was just thinking about meeting your family. You said they were excited to do that, but what if they don't care for me?" He told her if he loved her, then they would. "I don't know what being in love with anyone would be like. I mean, I loved my parents, but I haven't been on a lot of dates to know the difference between wanting sex or just wanting to be with a person."

Fisher couldn't help it, he burst out laughing. When she laughed as well, he smiled at her. Taking her hand into his, he kissed the back of it and held it while he drove one handed for a few minutes. He needed to think of the right words to say to her before speaking.

"I'm in love with you. I have been since I first understood you were my mate. You make me feel good about myself. I don't have a very high self-esteem. Not really." He glanced at her again. "I understand about you not being sure of the feelings I have for you. I can only hope you have the same for me someday soon. I will do my best to show you in so many ways that I love you. Daily. Hourly, if need be. Also, along with that, I want you to know that my parents and the rest of my family will love you as much as I do if they don't already. They're so excited to meet you I wouldn't be surprised if they were planning a big dinner for when we get home tonight to welcome you."

"I hope so. I mean, as I said, I've come to this with a great deal of baggage. You've taken care of one of the issues I had. I'm ever so grateful for you to have done that. I thought I was going to have to write off Mr. Alexander's money as a loss." He told her it was his profound pleasure. "Wow, that is a great deal of pleasure. I wish we could have sex soon. I know that we've tried to several times, but people keep coming around. It was wonderful that Peter was able to tell us that my brother and sister were coming around. I can't believe we got packed up that quickly and were on the road in less than ten minutes."

"I want to have sex with you too. But I really want to make love with you. I find that much better than just having sex." She told him she wouldn't know. Laughing again, he pulled off the highway to get gas and asked her if she wanted anything while he was out. "I mean, it's going to be a very long ride from here to home. Perhaps you can pick us up some snacks or something to munch on."

Handing her his credit card, he wasn't sure she was going to take it. When she did, putting it in her purse, he made sure she didn't see his sigh of relief.

While pumping the gas, he heard from Harper. She had a lot of information for him that she'd been looking for since the last time he spoke to her.

*First of all, the house you guys are going to be living in is amazing. I was by there yesterday, and I'm in love with it. Even Bryant thinks it's a perfect match for you. Okay. I've been doing some research on the family. The sister, Mary, isn't so much in the hole with money, but she's been stealing it from her husband's company for some time now. Not millions, as I thought, but hundreds of thousands. She has a serious gambling habit that is going to get her into deeper trouble than just with her husband. Mary owes some seriously pissed off people a lot of dough.* He asked if her husband had found out yet. *Yes, just a couple of days ago. I didn't have anything to do with it, but he figured it out when his partner called and told him they might not be able to meet their payroll without dipping into their own savings accounts. I guess after talking to their daughter, he's been trying to reach Mary for the last couple of days. He is not a happy camper.*

*No, I doubt he is. What about her brother? I'm assuming he's in a bit of trouble himself.* She said he was being hunted by the Feds. *The scam he was running. Yes, you told me about it. What's changed? I'm assuming something has.*

*Yes. And you're not going to like this any more than you did a couple of months ago when you figured out others were doing the same. Both of them have borrowed against their children's college funds. I told you that. What I didn't tell you was that they've also taken out credit cards in both their names, as well as a couple of loans, none of which have been repaid. So far, Rachel has a credit score of about two hundred. Peter's isn't a great deal* better at only two thirteen. *They're screwed as far as ever being able to purchase a home unless they can prove they had nothing to do with their parents doing this to them. It'll be a hard sell, I think.*

*Is there a way their creditors can be paid off? I mean, if we make a deal with them that we take care of this, will they back off from trying to hurt Piper, you think?* Harper told him she didn't have any idea. *I'd like to resolve this without bloodshed. If you could find out what you can from someone, I'd like to have a meeting with the four of them: the family and their spouses. Otherwise, someone, if not both of them, is going to jail. I'd like nothing better than to have it so we're not looking over our shoulders for the rest of our lives.*

*I'll see what I can do. Mostly, the best you can hope for is that after paying them off, they don't get into this kind of trouble again. However, I don't think that is going to keep them out of jail. Especially Louis. He's been scamming people, and paying them off might lessen his jail time, but it's not going to negate it.* Fisher told her he understood that. *Good. I'll see what I can find out and tell you when you get home tonight. I've had someone go through the house for you and fill it out. Your mom was happy to do it. There will be magic on the cabinets as well as the fridge that will keep it filled with the things you wish. If you ever want that to stop, just tell Peter.*

*I'll talk to Piper about it when we get home. I think she's taking this very well, but that might be just a little too much.* Harper laughed. *She's coming out of the store now, so I'll wait for you to give me the rest when we get home. As it stands right now, it should be around four when we get there. We left as soon as we heard her family was coming to talk to her.*

*Be careful. I don't know what sort of crap they're going to try, but I don't want either of you hurt. Okay?* He promised her he'd be as careful as she was. *That's what I want to hear. I'll figure this out and get back to you about it. Have a safe trip.*

Fisher thought about the meeting between Aurora and Piper. He'd not asked about it, not even to know how they had come together. It was her story, and she'd either tell him, or she'd tell him it was none of his business. Fisher had an idea she'd be a great deal more vocal about it if she didn't want him to know.

He could look, he supposed, but that just didn't seem right, on so many levels. There were so many things he wanted to do, to show her, but he figured overwhelming her once again wouldn't be helpful in the long run. It would be, he hoped, better if he simply waited until she asked.

"I got us some juice. I haven't any idea why I would need it, but Peter told me I needed to start drinking more of it all the time." He got into the truck when she did. "Did you know Snowflake and Peter are related? He said they were from the same spring. I had to ask what that had to do with anything. They were born in the same spring when the queen needed more faeries for the world. I think that's kind of sweet. What happens if she misses a couple of flowers? I mean, it does happen, right?"

"It does. Those faeries grow up to be bigger than their

siblings. Most of them go into the real world—not that being with the queen isn't real—but they work in places like the courthouse and other places to make sure paperwork is filed when it needs to be. Like our birth certificates are updated all the time by one of them, just so no one will realize we're as old as we are." Piper told him that was a wonderful idea. "They have other functions. Some of them are forever keeping an eye on children born to a family that isn't making it, or if there is violence there. We, as magical creatures, have managed to save a few of them. Not nearly as many as we'd like."

"That's wonderful." She looked out the front window of his truck as they pulled onto the highway. "That's how I met Aurora. I didn't know who she was at the time, other than someone who would bring food by when Mom and I were running low. A couple of times, she even picked up Mom's medication and brought it to us. When Mom died, I called for her, over and over, to come and stay with me. To be there for me. But she never came. She didn't even bother telling me why she couldn't be there with me. She just didn't come around anymore."

"Is that why you were so upset with her?" Piper told him that it had been. "Did she tell you why she'd not done as you wanted?"

"She didn't know. The hospital, she told me, is many levels of metal and concrete, so she'd not felt Mom's death as she might have if she'd been at our camper. Mom loved the outdoors, and she'd spend as much time as she could sitting out in the sun. That was how we met her. Aurora told us she'd been out walking and came upon us. It wasn't until she showed up at the camper last night that I even knew she was magical. I just thought she was just a woman who enjoyed the outdoors as much as we did. I didn't know how right I was until now."

The two of them spoke all the way back home, mostly about how he'd become what he was now, a cat that could shift into a man. How he'd been around for a long time, and how he had money. She told him she didn't hate her brother and sister, but she didn't like them at all. They had not just done her wrong, but mostly their parents. Just going on as if they'd not raised them or kept them safe and fed all the years they were growing up.

Fisher learned a great deal about her. She'd not had it very easy, but she told him she'd never trade getting to spend time with her parents in their final days for any reason. As soon as they stopped for gas again, he told her they could get some lunch and take a walk. Fisher wanted her to see his cat, something she'd been asking him for since they started out. He just hoped he didn't scare her too much. But he also knew that now was not the time. He'd show her his true self when they were home.

# *Chapter 5*

Paddy hung up the phone and sat staring at it as he thought of all the things he wanted to say to his wife. She'd ruined them both financially, as well as him mentally. This was putting such a strain on his mind that he'd been popping pain medication for his headache since he'd spoken to his partner three days ago. Mary had a great deal to answer for.

When he'd first found out that she'd been skimming — Not even close to what she'd been doing, but for now, calling it skimming made him feel better. But she'd been skimming money from the business bank accounts for months without either him or his partner knowing. Charlie said he'd suspected that was what she was doing, but with the huge merger coming up then, he'd forgotten to look. By the time he had looked, it was well into bankruptcy territory. Without going public about the loss to their company, there was no way they were going to be able to hide this for much longer.

"Mr. Benton, there is a man by the name of Bryant Prince here to speak to you. He said it's very urgent." Paddy told her to tell him he was out. "I'm afraid that won't work, sir. He told me he knows you're trying to contact your wife and the reason behind it. I wasn't aware you were trying to contact Mary, sir. I could have done that for you."

"It's all right, Connie. Just tell Mr. Prince I'll speak to him. Send him in." It startled him to see such a large man come through his doors. For whatever reason, Paddy had it in his head that this was one of the many people his wife owed, and he was here to kill him for the money. When the man smiled, Paddy felt no relief from it. "May I help you?"

"No, sir. I'm going to help you. At least my brother is. His name is Fisher Prince. And while that means nothing at all to you, he's going to be marrying your sister-in-law Piper soon. He wants to assure you that he's going to help you in any way he can."

Paddy laughed and asked if he was going to lend him three-hundred-thousand dollars. Instead of answering him, the man reached into his jacket pocket and pulled out what looked like a checkbook. Asking him who he was to make the check out to, Bryant filled out the amount and signed his name to the check as he waited.

"I was joking." Bryant said Fisher wanted to do this. "I can't take money from a stranger. I don't care who he says he's marrying. I don't even know how you figured out I was in trouble here. Is it already out in the papers?"

"Not that I'm aware of, no. I found out from your wife in an indirect way, but she's the one that took the money. Fisher and our whole family wants to help you out, so perhaps Mary will stop pursuing Piper about money that no longer exists. The money is gone from her mother's estate, sir. It went to pay all the bills that were acquired when Mrs. James was ill. They lost the house and cars, along with any chance of either of them getting the sort of health care that was needed." Paddy asked about the money they sent to Piper. "I wasn't told there had been any money sent to her from anyone in her family. I can check on that. But I'm sure that had there been any, Piper would have mentioned it. I don't know if you're aware of this or not, but Mary and Louis have been chasing Piper all over this end of the United States to get the money they feel is due to them. Four fifths of whatever was left. They seem to think that since Piper lived at the home, she doesn't deserve any proceeds from the money. The brother and sister seem to think that because they were married and had families, they should get a share for both them and their spouses."

"That's ridiculous. Why would I think Piper shouldn't have gotten anything she wanted out of whatever was leftover? She did all the work and gave up her life to make sure that Mary and Louis didn't have to worry about their parents." Bryant told him that wasn't the way he'd heard it. Paddy laughed. "After today, sir, I've no doubt at all that my wife is trying to get something for nothing, and would blame it all on her sister. What is the story she is telling Piper? Who I like, by the way. Never seen a person so opposite of her siblings."

"Both Louis and Mary seem to think Piper should have stayed home with the parents, as she was already living there when the father became ill. Then after he died, it was left to her to care for her mother too. Money wasn't as tight as it was at the end. Begging for money from Mary and Louis had become a lost cause. From what I'm to understand, neither of them even came to visit their mother in the ten years after their father passed. They were even late to the funeral. It's not my family, but I would think they'd just leave her alone for all she did for them when there was no one else." Paddy had known there was more to the funeral than Piper giving them the wrong time just to be mean. He asked Bryant how much he knew about his wife. "I know she and Louis are in Tennessee at the moment. That was the last place Piper was before she started making her way to her home with my brother. Louis has purchased a gun. I've no idea what he plans to do with it, but he has it. They started home, Fisher and Piper, to avoid any trouble from them. Fisher wanted me to come here and see if you think paying back the money Mary took will be enough to keep Mary away from Piper."

"I wish I could tell you something you want to hear, Bryant, but I just don't know anymore. She has a problem. And I don't know if you paying the debt she made for my company will keep her from doing it again. It would be deeply appreciated, but I think she'll continue with what she has in her head no matter what I do on my end." Bryant handed the check to him. "I don't know if taking this is a good idea."

"You've been honest with me, Paddy, and I'll do the same for you. If she hurts even a single hair on Piper's head, she will be ended." Bryant stood up, and Paddy did as well. "I take being related to Piper very seriously. She makes my brother laugh and smile. And they're in love. But if Mary doesn't stop with this and gets to the point of harming one of my family, I'm afraid there will be nothing I can do to save her."

"I don't know what to say." Bryant put out his hand, and Paddy took it. "I'm calling the police right now. I don't want her dead, and I'm sure you don't want that either. But she's done enough damage now that it's impossible for me to trust her word that she's going to stop before it's too late."

"It is too late, I'm afraid. You should check into your son's credit history. You might be surprised by what you find there. As well as for Rachel. Piper loves both her niece and nephew, but they're also going to suffer in ways you'll soon be made aware of." Paddy sat down again, hard. "Also, I'm afraid their scholarships are gone. My wife is looking into how they managed to get into the money for that. If you're interested, I'll be happy to pass on the news. But I'm afraid it's going to get them into more trouble than either of them can buy off this time."

"You knew this when you offered the money. That even with you helping me with my company, they'd still be in deep shit." Bryant said he had. "Why? Why would you come in here and write me a check for that much money when you knew Mary was still going to have to go to jail?"

"Because, as I said, Piper is family. And she loves the kids of her family. Fisher also hopes that since he helped you out, you'll still be a part of her family." Paddy told him, of course, he would. "Good. I'm very glad to hear that. There isn't any reason in the world why your company has to suffer because your wife made a few life changing choices without your knowledge. No matter how this turns out, you still have your son to think of."

Thanking him again, Paddy pulled up a credit history on his son. Staring at the report, it occurred to Paddy that the date of his son's first bad credit report was only a few days after he'd turned five. As he read through the list, he estimated his son had racked up nearly a million dollars in debt, all before he'd graduated from middle school. Paddy was sure the only reason it wasn't more was because his rating had fallen so far down the chart.

Paddy started making a list of things he needed to take care of. First and foremost, he was going to call the credit bureau and have them look into Peter's credit. After that, he started doing searches on other things. Like how much the debt was that Mary Margaret, Mary's mother, had at the time of her death.

When his phone rang again, he picked it up without

looking to see who it might have been. He heard Mary telling someone she was calling her husband now.

"Paddy? Are you there?" He told her he was. "Good. You're not going to believe this, but I've some trouble here in New Jersey. I was doing a little shopping, and they're saying my credit card is no longer any good. I might have been a little more upset about it than I should have been. They've had me arrested. I need you, honey. I need you to help me. Losing my mother has been difficult on me, as you know."

"Do I? Know how you've suffered, Mary? The last thing I heard about you was that you were down in Tennessee trying to get poor Piper to give you something she doesn't have. Money. It's always money with you, isn't it? Don't lie to me again about where you are. I know exactly where you and your brother are." She told him she didn't know what he was talking about, but that she'd meant to say she was in Ohio. "All right. Then can you tell me where the three-hundred-thousand dollars is that was in our business checking account? Or perhaps why Peter has a terrible credit score when I know for a fact he's never had a credit card for the health spa that you go to?"

"I don't know what you're talking about, Paddy. Can't we discuss then when I get home? I have such a headache, and I'm exhausted. I've not been sleeping well since my — "

"Yes, since your mother died. When was the last time you saw her alive, Mary? You told me you were seeing her once a month or more if you could swing it. From what

I've heard, you've not once seen your mother in all the time she was ill. When that was mentioned at the funeral, you assured me that Piper was trying to make you feel bad for not being on time. I should have spoken to you then about it. Also, you've not once seen her since your father died." Mary asked him what his point was. "My point? Well, I guess you might as well know my point now. I'm not bailing you out. You've taken enough from me and my son. Also, you might find this as a surprise, but I'm calling the police as soon as I hang up from talking to you. I've had enough. As for your credit card? They've all been canceled. In trying to reach you by phone to talk to you about the missing money, I had it in my head that you'd call if you couldn't gamble anything more away. Lucky me, I guess. That's just what you did."

"Paddy, I've told you I've been arrested, and here you are talking to me about gambling and taking money. If you are going to cut back, please don't do it to me without asking me first. I'm not going to be upset this time, but turn the credit cards on, and I'll forgive you." He didn't say anything to her. "Paddy? Did you hear what I said? I have to get home for you, and the only way that is going to happen is if you come to get me or I have the credit cards reinstated so I can pay the fine here. I don't know why you're making this so complicated."

"I'm not going to do anything for you, Mary. As of right now, I'm washing my hands of you." She told him he was just upset. "I am at that. Very much so. You've lied and cheated me for the very last time. I'm finished with you. Don't come here if you manage to get home. The locks will be changed, and the staff will know not to allow you in my home again."

Hanging up on her felt good. Of course, as usual, after sitting there thinking about what he'd said to her, Paddy felt terrible. Just as he was going to pick up the phone to make a call to the jail to get her out, Peter walked into the room.

When his son had been born, Paddy could have taken on the world. He grew into a wonderful toddler, then a teenager. Peter had never been into any real trouble. Even though they'd given him a car, Paddy knew he'd not been in trouble with the law. Peter's grades were always on top, and when he graduated from high school in a few weeks, he'd be valedictorian.

"What's up, son?" Peter grinned at him and sat down across from him. "I was thinking the two of us should go and get some dinner tonight. Your mother is out, and I don't know when she'll be back. What do you think?"

"I think you have bad news for me, and you're going to butter me up before you tell me. I'm an adult, Dad. How about if you learn to pull the Band-Aid off and just tell me what it is." Paddy felt his eyes fill with unshed tears. "Dad, you're starting to scare me. What's happened? What has you so upset?"

Paddy told him about everything, from the money his mother took to the way she'd fucked with Peter's credit.

He told him about how she told him she was in Ohio and shopping. Paddy even told his son about Piper and Fisher getting married. Also, the money Fisher had given him to settle the business accounts.

"That wasn't anything I expected. You're not going to bail her out, are you, Dad? I mean, she's my mom, sure. But if you left her there for a while, it wouldn't bother me a bit." Paddy told him he was going to file for divorce. "It's about time. I wish you'd done it years ago. Mom makes you sad and tense. I've been coming home for the last few months worried I was going to find you in this room dead from a stress related heart attack."

"I feel like I've been running a marathon and never could get past the first hill. But this thing with Charlie. If Fisher hadn't stepped in, we would have been screwed." Peter told him he was sorry. "Don't be, son. It's not your fault. But I can't do this with your mother anymore. I've tried over and over to get her help. She'll be all right for a couple of weeks, then it's like her mind explodes or something, and she needs to go and nearly lose the house over her habit. Or sickness. I'm not sure what to call it. But whatever it is, I just can't afford to take it on any longer."

"I don't blame you at all, Dad. You're right. Mom is out of control." He looked so sad that Paddy wanted to get up and hug him. Then he wondered if men hugged their sons anymore. "She's messed up my college. I was looking forward to being able to go there and not have to work."

"Peter, having the scholarship was a wonderful thing,

but I can still afford to pay for you going to any college you want. I'd never take that dream away from you." He said his mom shouldn't have been able to either. "You're right about that. I'm going to see an attorney in the morning about your credit score too. We'll get through this. I promise."

"Dad, do you think Piper really is getting married? I hope so. I hope she has a brood of kids too. She's about the sweetest aunt a person could have. I can't wait to meet her husband to be." He told him how he'd like his brother. "Yes, well, I'm going to the wedding. No matter what kind it is. She's been there for me when I needed a woman to talk to. Piper did a lot for this family, and I, for one, am not going to have her heart broken by my mom ever again."

"I agree." Once Paddy said he'd be ready in twenty minutes to go out to dinner, Peter went up to his room to change. Paddy made three phone calls and deposited the check into the business account. Modern technology made it easy for him to just snap a photo and have it in the bank. Then he called his partner to let him know the money was in the account.

Tomorrow was going to be a good day. Paddy wasn't sure how that was going to happen, but he was determined to make it work for him. He realized while waiting for the secretary to get him an appointment that he didn't feel the least bit upset about getting a divorce. In fact, he was happy for it. Thrilled, no less.

~*~

Buck was keeping an eye on dinner for his Sara and also keeping an eye on the front door so that when his son came in, he'd be the first to meet his new daughter. To him, they were daughters and not in-laws. He had a feeling that Fisher and Piper might be the best thing since his wife's homemade grape jelly.

"Buck, what are you doing?" He smiled at his wife, and she tisked at him. "You're supposed to be watching dinner for me, not snooping around to see when Fisher gets back. My goodness, you act as if you've never had a daughter-in-law before. Help me shuck this corn."

He did so but didn't stop looking at the front door. Sara was telling him about the corn, how it was the last of the season, though he knew if they wanted corn year-round, the little faeries would make it happen.

The front door made a sound, and he jumped up, dumping silky corn hair all over the floor.

"Don't you dare leave this mess on the floor, Buck Prince. She might be out there, and I'll not have her thinking I'm a terrible housekeeper." Doing just what she wanted him to do, Buck was wondering how much longer he was going to have to wait. "They'll be here when they get here, you old buzzard. Just calm down before you scare her off."

He mumbled that he wanted to be the first to greet her. "You know, welcome her to the family. It's not fair that everyone usually meets people before I do." Sara asked him how old he was. "I don't rightly know anymore. Why does my age matter right now?"

"Because I'd swear you're a five-year-old without a nap. Gotta meet her first. Well, I have news for you, dummy, she's met the only man in the world that is going to mean everything to her. And we're just going to have to deal with it." Buck looked at his wife. When she turned her back to him, he went to her and turned her so he could see the tears on her face. "I'm not sure why I'm upset. But this is the first daughter-in-law that's come to us that isn't being hunted down like a dog by her family. They might not care for her, but she's not going to be killed off by any of them."

"Why would that make you cry, Sara? Do you want her to be hurt?" She smacked him on the forehead. "Then I have no idea why you're crying like you are. Perhaps if you explained it to me, you won't have to hurt your pretty hand by smacking me around like a turnip."

"I have nothing in common with the others." He didn't understand and told her that. "They're so wonderfully smart and have businesses to go to. I have this house and making dinner once in a while when they come over."

"Why don't you have a job? I mean, you don't have to work, but I don't see any reason for you not to go and find yourself something to do if you want. I thought you was working on that there place that runs charity things." She told him it wasn't for all the time. "Why not? I mean, why don't you work on it all the time? It sure would be bigger and bring in more stuff if you did it all the time instead of rushing things along in one month, don't you think?"

"Yes, but what would I do about the house?" He didn't know what she meant, so he asked her why she'd want to be stuck in the house all day. "I don't want to be. Not all the time. But this is where they can find me if they want me."

"Oh honey, I think you're all mixed up about something. You need to push your way into what they're doing. I'm thinking they have it in their heads that you're a homebody, and they don't want to take that away from you. You know, get you out of the house because you're here." He knew that it had sounded messed up, but Sara smiled at him, and he felt he'd done something right. "The next time you want to have lunch or go shopping, just call one of them up and tell them they're going with you. Or all of them. I'm sure if you start it, they'll understand you want to be out and about like they are."

"Do you think so?" He told her he was sure of it. "Then I'm going to do it. I'm also going to try and be a lot more assertive when I'm around them."

Buck wasn't sure that was anything he wanted to witness. He thought his little wife was about as assertive as he wanted her to be. But if it made her happy, he'd be happy too. A smile from Sara could make him feel as happy as a toad on the pond.

When the door opened behind him, Buck stayed working on the mess he'd made. Sara dried her hands and made her way into the hall to see who it might be. He knew it was his son, Fisher, but didn't want to take this from Sara. She needed to be there first a great deal more than he did. He turned around after tossing the hair away to look at the woman standing next to his son.

"My goodness gracious. You're more beautiful than Fisher told us." She flushed a pretty shade of red, which only made her more beautiful to him. "I'm Buck Prince. This here is my wife, Sara. Welcome to the family, Piper."

Sara hugged her first, then Buck did. He noticed that Fisher was standing back like he was waiting for someone to notice him. Hugging his son, Fisher hugged him back like he'd been gone for months instead of a couple of days. Standing back and looking at his son, he could see that he was about as in love with his pretty mate as Buck was with his own. Fisher in love was something that Buck had never thought to happen.

"You all right, son?" Fisher hugged him again. "I'm taking that as a yes. You didn't have any trouble getting back, did you? I mean, I know someone is looking for Piper."

"No, no trouble at all. I'm sort of trying to get her family to back off of Piper so she can have a good life. I don't know how much you know, but her sister is in jail, and the police are looking for her brother right now. He's going in for a Ponzi scam, I guess." Buck told him that Bryant and Harper had told them. "Yes, well, I helped out her brother-in-law and he's taken things a little further along in filing for divorce. Also, his wife, Mary, is going to have to explain how she got the money she stole."

"Well, you know we're all here for the two of you. You only have to ask, and we'll band together like we usually do." Fisher told him he knew that too. "Good. The rest of them aren't going to come over until six. I told them that would give the two of you time to get settled in after driving all that way. You been by your house yet?"

"We drove by it on the way here. I dropped off her camper so that Peter and Snowflake can get started on it for an office for her. She's a computer programmer." Buck knew what it meant to be that, but not what it really entailed. Computers had been around a long time, but he'd never taken to them. "I also wanted to get with you and Mom about a couple of things I've noticed while down in the Smoky area. Investments that might help out some of the poorer neighborhoods down there. Also, for the park."

"I'd be glad to help out with whatever you're thinking about." Fisher said they'd talk after dinner. "All right then. Come on now, son, let's get ourselves a little bit to drink. Your momma, she's been cooking most of the day away, waiting on the two of you."

Buck listened to Piper telling Sara about her job and the things she'd been working on with it. He laughed when she told them about the man who'd not paid his bill and what she'd done to him. Also about how she loved having a faerie around to keep her on point.

"I've so much going through my head right now that I'm having a hard time focusing on one single task. I do need to get back to work soon. With my mom passing away recently, it's been hard on me to try and get my ducks in a row, so to speak." Buck told her she had plenty of time to get back to work, and she smiled at him. "Fisher said you and your wife were the nicest people he knew. He also said you'd welcome me with open arms. I'm so very glad I've come here. Fisher and I, we're getting to know each other, but I've had such a wonderful time with him so far."

"Good for you. Fisher is one of the best. All my sons are." She said she'd not met the others yet. "You will. They'll be here for dinner soon. We're loud and argue a great deal, but we love with all that we are. You're going to see that tonight. And know that you're as safe here as you've ever been in your life. They'll do good by you."

"Fisher is helping out my in-laws. I didn't ask him to do that. I want you to know he did that all on his own." Buck stared at her a moment, then smiled. "You don't believe me. Do you?"

"I do. You just made this old man so much more proud of my son than I've already been. He did do that, didn't he? That's what we do. We help out others that might need a hand up. It doesn't matter to us why that happened so long as they're not thieves or cutthroats. We, as a family, do what we can no matter what. Thank you for telling me that." She nodded at him. "I'm thinking you're confused. I don't blame you none. I don't. But you're a good girl, and we're mighty glad to have you as a part of our family."

"Thank you. I think I'm mighty glad to be a part of this family too." They both laughed, and Buck felt pretty good about the girl. She was a beautiful woman too. One that would keep his son on his toes, no doubt about that.

He was right proud of his boys when they showed up. Buck and Sara had wanted them to be boys they could let go in the world and not have them embarrass them any. When they met their new sister, each of them treated her with the respect she deserved and even managed to get her scent while they were at it. There wasn't a better family around as far as he was concerned.

When they were set to sit down and have some food together, he nearly wept when they stood up until their momma sat down. He also knew as soon as dinner was over, each and every one of them would go into the kitchen and clean up without nary a thought to letting their momma do it. Yes, sir. Buck was right proud of his children.

# Chapter 6

The house was much larger than he thought they'd need. With each room they went into, the more he thought Piper was overwhelmed. Coming from living in a camper for such a long time, being in this much room would make anyone feel lost. Finally, she turned to him.

"I'd like to go to the kitchen, please." There was desperation there. Fisher thought even Peter could hear it. Nodding, he took her hand into his and moved toward the stairs. "It's very beautiful, isn't it? I mean, the house is like everything I'd ever dreamed of living in."

Fisher could almost feel the relief from the faeries. They scattered then, taking flight to different rooms to no doubt decorate them to whatever they found in her mind. It was funny to him. He'd been living in an apartment for so long it had taken him a minute or two to get used to the size of the house. He couldn't imagine how bad it was for Piper.

Once in the kitchen, she didn't sit as he'd thought she

would, but fussed around the kitchen, from making a cup of tea, which he knew she didn't drink all that often, to looking in the cabinets then closing them up.

"This is really freaking me out." Fisher told her he could see that. "I love this house. Everything about it. But the fact that it's everything I thought of in a house is sort of like having someone in my mind all the time. Is that how they knew what I'd like?"

"Yes. They didn't mean to be intrusive." She said she knew that. "Good. I don't know when they'll start decorating the rooms—I'd say they're doing it now—but they've gotten ideas straight from your head. Are you going to be all right with that?"

"So if I were to think of a pool in the back yard, I'd only have to go and look, and it would be there?" He nodded and got up to look out the window over the sink. Seeing the pool there, he sat back down. "I don't want to look. I'm sure it's there, but I'm not going to look. I love to swim. As a cat, do you hate the water?"

"No. I actually love swimming too. Even my cat enjoys it. Are you all right?" She told him she wasn't sure. "Yes, I can see that. Just take a deep breath and tell me what you want to do about the faeries. They only have your best interest at heart. You know that, don't you?"

"I do. And it's so sweet that they want to please me like this. Are they going to change things around every time I have a different idea about a room?" Fisher laughed and told her he didn't know for sure. "Yes, well, we might have to talk to someone in charge about that."

"You do realize you're in charge of them while they're in the house, don't you?" She just stared at him. "I've overwhelmed you again, haven't I?"

"I feel like I've been tossed the best things in life, and I'm not sure if someone is going to come along and tell me it was all a joke and that it's not real. It is real, isn't it, Fisher? I mean, just because I'm a little stressed out, it doesn't mean you're going to tell me you don't love me, are you?" He told her he'd never do that. "I'm happy to hear that. Because I've fallen in love with you. I don't know when it happened, but I only just realized I've been in love with you since you spoke to me in the middle of the night."

"I have loved the thought of you since I was old enough to realize I'd have a mate at some point in my life. But since meeting you, holding you, I've realized that none of my thoughts about what it might be like were ever close to the real thing. You are, without a doubt, the best thing that has ever happened to me." She came to him and wrapped her arms around his shoulders. "I love you, Piper. Will you marry me?"

"Yes." He sat her down on the table and got down on one knee. "Oh, I so love your parents right now. For teaching you the correct way to woo a woman, and to be the most romantic person I've never known."

He pulled the ring out of his pocket. Aurora had helped him put the beautiful amethyst into a ring. Not only was the gem on the top, but she had fashioned a band to go with it that had the gem circle it in a beautiful pattern of alternating diamond and the dark purple of the stone itself.

"I don't know what will come with this ring. The others got magic that surpassed what they already had. Then again, there might not be anything more with it than my undying love." He put it onto her finger, pushing it up to her knuckle. It fit around her like it had been made to fit on the first try. "I love you with all of my heart. I will keep you safe and from any harm for the rest of our lives together."

Looking up at Piper when she moaned, he saw her body stiffen, her head thrown back as great spikes of light came from her. The color wasn't white, as he had expected, but every shade of purple that he could have imagined. When she looked down at him, her eyes were bright too. The color of the amethyst on her finger paled by the new color of her eyes.

She said his name twice before he was able to stand. Whatever was happening to her, it was doing the same to him. Reaching blindly for Piper, filling his hands with her flesh, in a passing thought, he realized that her skin wasn't hot as he had expected it to be, but cold. Like the frozen ponds he'd skated on as a child.

Fisher woke in bed. It took him several minutes to remember what had happened and how he'd gotten here. Sitting up slowly, his body aching in a way he'd not felt for a very long time, he looked at the woman beside him.

Piper seemed to have weathered better than he had. He told her how sore he was.

"I am as well. I was just lying here thinking about getting up to pee, but my body tells me it's not ready for that sort of movement." He laid back down. "You have a streak of white in your hair. I don't remember seeing that before."

He looked at her. "You do as well. It's bright white. Not gray, but a shiny white." He touched it with his fingers and smiled at her. "It's soft. Like silk running through my fingers. Or even a waterfall that comes from a high mountain top in the middle of summer. We have one, by the way — a watering hole. As cats, we can go there and play around. There isn't any worry of anyone being around, so we might end up there all day."

"I think it's a tad cold for that now, don't you?" He wouldn't care if there was a foot of snow on the ground if she had wanted to go now. Fisher would have given her the world if she asked him for it. Leaning down, he was so close to kissing her when she stopped him. "If you kiss me now, I'm going to strip you down and rape you. I've had enough interruptions and people coming around asking for shit to last several lifetimes."

"Are you telling me you want me to kiss you, or are you telling me you don't? Right now I feel like you're telling me you do, but I don't want to assume — "

She pulled him down to her and kissed him deliciously. Touching his fingers over her breast to her belly, he told her how to be naked for him. As he made his way up to her throat, she was naked beneath him. Fisher thought the same thing and felt his cock touching her thigh. It took all his control, willing himself to slow down and not take her right this second.

"I'm betting there are all kinds of things I'm going to learn from you, aren't there?" Fisher asked her what she meant just before taking her hard nipple into his mouth. "What did I ask you? I suddenly can't remember."

Laughing a little, he took her nipple into his mouth again and then suckled it as hard as he dared. Her fingers raking through his hair had him rolling until he was settled between her legs, his cock hard and pulsing, ready to take her as quickly and as hard as he could. But he knew he'd have to pleasure her first.

She was so responsive to everything he did to her. Touching her flesh would have her moaning loudly. Running his tongue over and around her nipple would make her breathe hard. Even when he slid his hand down to her knee, she cried out, telling him it was too much, then asked him for more as it hadn't been enough.

Fisher had the same effect from her touches. He thought her greedy at one point, then too slow to touch him in the next breath. When she wrapped her warm hand around his cock, it was all he could do not to come in her hand, spewing his cum all over her belly and breasts.

"I need you, Fisher. I don't just want you, but I need you inside of me." Happy to oblige her, he slid into her heat when she removed her hand. She guided him to her warmth and took him into her. "Yes. That's it, that's what I needed."

He didn't move, fearful he'd come too quickly, spoil her fun of riding him. Rolling to his back, Fisher helped her over him, his cock deep inside of her. Holding her hips until she hit her stride, he watched her face as she rode him. There couldn't have been anything more beautiful, all-consuming than Piper riding his cock, Fisher thought.

When she leaned down to his chest, he held her to him. Her tongue rolling over his nipple was more than he could handle. Barely able to hold onto his own needs, Fisher lost all control when she bit down on his nipple.

"Christ, yes." He filled her with himself, surging upward, over and over, until he thought he'd die from the pleasure. Even after coming before her, Fisher needed more, wanted to watch her face as she came with him. Rolling her over, pressing her into the mattress as he fucked her, he cupped her ass tightly in his hands to be as deep inside of her as he could. "Come for me, love. Come with me, and I'll be yours forever."

Piper didn't just come, she exploded. Her body stiffening under his was all the warning he got when suddenly her nails dug into his shoulder, her legs wrapped around him like a tightly pulled string. As she screamed out her release, screaming to him that she was in love with him, Fisher watched her face and was enchanted with her beauty once again.

His own climax took him nearly to unconsciousness. It swept over him like a fast moving storm. Holding onto Piper was all he could do so he'd not fly apart, not break into millions of pieces like the stars that were behind his eyelids. Coming a third, then a fourth time, Fisher dropped down on top of Piper even as she closed her eyes too.

Opening his eyes, he could see the room was darker than before. Untangling himself from Piper was hard to do—he never wanted to leave the warmth of her arms. He got up and looked out the window before he closed the curtain.

Fisher stared hard at what he was seeing to try and make his mind make out what he was actually seeing. When Piper came up behind him, wrapping her arms around his waist, he pulled her around to stand in front of him, facing the yard.

"Tell me I'm seeing what I think I'm seeing." Piper laughed, then started for the door. "Piper, you're naked."

He dressed himself and left too, noticing that before she opened the front door, Piper had finally dressed. Not that he didn't enjoy seeing her naked. But they were headed to the yard, and there was no telling who else might be out and about this evening.

"It's snow." He laughed as she laid down in the quickly deepening stuff. "I've never seen it before. Look how soft it is. Oh, I can make a snowman. I've never made one of those either."

Fisher didn't bother going to her but sat on the steps

leading to the wraparound porch as she played like a child. His cat was itching to play with her, and suddenly Fisher thought what the hell.

He'd never known a time when he felt so good, not just because he was in love with Piper but because he actually did feel free. Standing in the snow, he let his cat take over, letting him be the cat he was. As he started leaping and pawing at it like Piper was, Fisher laughed along with Piper.

They were both glad for the full moon. It let them play in the yard for longer than he thought they might have had it been anything else. Even after Piper tired of her antics, his cat seemed to enjoy himself even more. Rolling around in the light stuff, his cat seemed to be like a cub rather than the thousands of year old cat he really was.

"Your white streak is more pronounced than it was when you were a man. It might just be the snow all over you." He moved toward her, her laughter making him smile. "I know you can't change me. I've been talking to the other women about this and that. Will making love with you be like that every time?"

*Christ, I hope so. But then again, we might be testing our immortality if it is. I thought you'd killed me a couple of times.* He laid his head on her legs and closed his eyes when she started scratching him behind the ears. *I thought you'd be afraid of me. I mean, I'm not exactly a small little kitten.*

"You are to me. When you were playing just now, all I could think of was that you're acting like one." She touched her finger to where he knew the white streak was. "It is more pronounced. I think it might be wider as well. Who do we speak to about this?"

*I would think Aurora.* The ground around them shook a little, and the faerie queen was standing in the yard with them. Aurora was a beautiful woman, but now he could see she looked exhausted. *We must have summoned you. I'm sorry, my lady. I'm sure you're very busy right now.*

"No, I came to the two of you with a purpose. And you could never call to me when I would not come to help you. You are, after all, my black tiger. I've come to tell you what you have received with the gem I gave you to share with Piper." She touched her fingers to his fur, and the warmth of it settled over his body. "You will have this for the rest of your lives. It will be the mark that will open doors for the two of you. I didn't know if it would come to you, but I'm ever so glad it did. The two of you will have great magic too."

"Excuse me, but I think I have more than I can handle now." Aurora laughed at Piper. "I don't think I like where this is going. Seriously, I'm having enough trouble trying to figure out my moving home, much less figuring out magic that is going to make me fearful of hurting someone."

"I understand that. I can help you with that, however. Both of you." He laughed when Piper asked her what that entailed, her concern showing enough suspicion in her tone there wasn't any way Aurora could have missed it. "I only need to touch you at the same time, and it will make it so every bit of magic you now have will be explained to you. Something like accelerated lessons."

"Isn't that the same as more magic?" Aurora laughed again. The worry lines that had been there were all but gone. "Your laughter reminds me of bells. Tiny ones that tinkle rather than chime. I'm sure you've been told that before."

"I have not. People are afraid to tell me what they think of me. I believe it stems from my ability to destroy whatever comes around." Piper asked her if she meant kill. "No. If I have to take something out, I will destroy it in a way that nothing remains. Nothing of their line or their story."

"That's a great deal to be scared about. I think I'd piss myself too if you were pissed with me. You're not, are you?" Aurora assured her she was not. "Good. One less thing I have to worry about right now. As for the lessons, I would love to know what I have and what to do to use it. If Fisher doesn't mind."

He didn't and told them both he would like to know too. Then before she touched him, he asked if he had to be man or beast. Aurora smiled at him before she answered, telling him his cat needed to be there.

Fisher wasn't sure why, but he was slightly nervous by her look. Then she touched them both on the head. Fisher knew it was the streak she was touching. After her touch, Fisher knew why she wanted him to be beast.

~*~

Piper sat on the couch after Aurora left and didn't move. Fisher had joined her at some point, but he too seemed to be shell shocked by what had happened in the yard. It was difficult for her to be upset by the chain of events, but Piper was reasonably sure that if she laughed right now, she'd never be able to stop. She'd be committed and never see the man she loved again.

"I could always hear extraordinarily well, but I'm sure I can hear a mosquito buzzing around a room several hundred miles away." Piper laughed at Fisher's comment, then put her hand over her mouth, stilling it before it got out of control. "Do you really think what she said about my tiger is true? That I'm twice the size I was before?"

"Yes. I saw you before and after." He nodded but didn't say anything more. "Fisher, what did she mean when she said we'd have several litters? I'm a person, not a cat."

"I don't think you're either one now. Do you? I mean, we were given some very powerful magic. I'm doubting even my brothers have this much if you were to bundle it all together." Piper asked him if he was all right. "No. I don't think I am. I have this loop going on in my head that keeps telling me I'm powerful. And that I'm the queen's protector. I don't even know how to protect you all the time, much less a queen that is all over the place."

"I can protect us both too." Fisher grinned at her. "What is that for? By the way, you sort of look like a fruitcake right now. Don't do that around your family, or they really will have you committed."

"I just thought of you protecting me. I don't think I've ever had anyone say that to me." She asked him if he thought her incapable of doing that. "No. On the contrary, I think you'd do a great job of keeping me out of trouble and safe. I'd gladly be your damsel in distress for you to help me."

"Don't be silly." She got up off her couch and went to sit with him. "I was just thinking that this couch needs to be deeper when we're on it together. That way, you can hold me while we watch the fireplace."

The couch widened under her, and she stretched out more. It should have freaked her out a little, having her every wish taken care of. But she was going with the flow now. Having things explained to her, along with the magic, Piper felt like she was on top of things. That she was able to understand more than she had previously. Turning to lie on her back, she looked up at Fisher.

"She said the streaks in our hair mark us as hers. I thought you all belonged to her." Fisher explained. "So this is more than her just creating you and your family as shifters. You and I literally belong to her and her castle. Do you think we'll get to go there someday? I have a feeling there are a lot of things around the castle that people no longer believe in."

"You mean like dragons and unicorns? They're there. Several of them, as a matter of fact. There are also flying horses, as well as a few animals that were here but have gone extinct. She told us once that if the humans learn to control themselves again, she might well bring them back. She's done it before, I guess." Piper was excited to know that. That Aurora worked with both worlds, hers and the one she lived in, to make sure that all animals had a chance. Piper asked Fisher about the flying horses. "They're beautiful creatures, but they're not as big as portrayed in books. Not small either, but about the size of a small horse. Their colors are wonderfully brilliant, as well. Like rainbows from the sky."

Piper loved talking to Fisher. There didn't seem to be any subject he didn't know at least a little about. Some things, jobs that he'd had in his past lives, he was more knowledgeable about, but he never talked down to her or made her feel stupid because she didn't know as much as he did.

"Once, when we were just coming to our own, becoming adult tigers, we happened upon a man with a traveling circus. He was down on his luck and having to cut corners wherever he went. But he was good to his animals. All of them loved him." Piper asked Fisher if he could speak to all animals. "Yes. I've been able to converse with all manner of creatures. I believe you can do that as well."

"I can, can't I?" Piper looked around the room to find something, anything she could test out her newfound powers on. When she didn't see anything, she asked Fisher to continue. "I want to hear about everything you've ever done. I want to be a part of every aspect of your life since you were born."

"That's a lot of stories. But back to the traveling circus. As I said, he was a good man. Just not doing as well as he hoped, I suppose. Traveling from town to town, he enjoyed meeting young people, telling about the creatures he had as well as anything else that he could impart to them. We followed him for a few days before Dad came up with a plan to help him out. It was dangerous, not to him but to us, but the need to help him was greater than our fear of being harmed."

She watched Fisher's face as he thought about that time in his life. She could almost see the younger him, watching a circus with caged animals. Piper wasn't sure she'd like something like that, to see animals being held with chains and ropes.

"One night, while the people were sitting around their fire, having the very last of their food, my dad, as a man, walked into the circle and told him who he was. Not his real name, of course—we were never to do that. He told him how he had these beautiful tigers that were all in good health and would listen to him when they did their antics. He never said tricks. We only did things that a normal tiger would do, you see." She nodded, fascinated by the story he was weaving in her mind. "Dad called for us, three at a time, so that we'd not be caged for too long, and had us do things like you'd do to impress someone. We would stand up or roll over, much to the amusement of the people there. We were hired on the spot. But Dad, he had a plan that would make the man enough money to see him through the winter. You see, that's all he had left. The poor man was in bad health, and wasn't going to have another season of being the only circus that had three black tigers in his show."

"What did you end up doing? I mean, the plan, what was it?" Fisher told her what his dad had done. Piper cried. "That is far and away the sweetest thing I've ever heard. Showing the man how to advertise and to make sure the next town would know they were coming so the townspeople saved their money to see the show. I loved your dad before this, but I love and respect him even more for what he did. You said the money went to those in the circus after he passed away. Did he have anyone left to take care that he was buried in a proper way?"

"Only you would think of that, my love. No, he had no one but the people that traveled with him. But they did him out right. With the money they'd made, a great deal back then, they not only bought him a proper headstone, but they had it carved with the likeness of him so all would remember such a great man." When he told her the name of the man, Piper realized she had heard of him and smiled. "We were put on this earth to help those in need. To help not just the creatures like us, but humans too. Only those with a kindness deep inside of them ever profited from our magic. Those that abused the power had the ruination of their lives set upon them until they were less than they'd been before."

"Do you do that still? I mean, go around helping people when you hear about it?" He explained to her how much easier it was now that there were computers. "I would imagine you can have about every person in the world at your fingertips if you know how to look. I can do that as well. Find people that might not want you to find them. Also, to write programs for large companies that wish to save their information from others."

"I don't know how to do that." She asked him what he meant. "Find certain people. Nor could any of us use the computer all that well until about ten years ago. We might well be magical, but things like computers aren't something we're all that good at."

She got up off the couch and made her way to his office. There was a computer in there. One of the faeries had asked if she wanted to help with putting the correct one in the room. Sitting there while it came on, she asked Fisher for a name of someone they'd helped, just as a starting point for her to show him what a computer could do for them.

"Try your brother. I have no idea why, but I'm betting you can find out more about him than Harper can with all her contacts." She pulled up her brother. It was the first time she'd ever done that to any of her family. Piper sat back in her chair when she saw the information there for her to get. "What is it, honey? I shouldn't have had you look up his name. I'm so sorry. Just go to someone else's name. Mine. Use mine."

"Louis has money." Fisher came around the side of

the desk to where she was sitting. "My parents, they put money in an account for all of us when we were children. It was a savings account just for children if I remember correctly. I remember being so proud of myself when she'd allow me to put my own money in. It's still there—all of it. It's right there for him. I have to look for Mary's account."

She had money too. More than Louis did, but not by a great deal. It had been sitting in the account, drawing interest since they'd been born. It looked as if the accounts had been opened a week almost to the day after Mom had given birth to them.

"Look to see if your account is still there." It was. Nothing close to what her sister and brother had, but there was a substantial amount in all their accounts. "What are you going to do with it? I'm sure it could go a long way in keeping their families in a better place after they're both in prison."

"I'm not going to tell them, first of all. If I do, they'll drain it just for the sole purpose of spending it on stupid shit. No, I'll tell their spouses about it." Fisher told her that was a great idea. "Yes, but after the families empty it out, then I'm going to tell them what Mom had done for them. They won't be happy, maybe, but they might be happier knowing that Mom had cared for them more than they thought."

"I don't know if you should tell them face to face." Piper asked him why not. "Because they'll be dead anyway if they so much as come at you. And while I don't know them as well as you do, you can bet this isn't going to be something they're going to be happy about. Especially since it'll be there then gone before they can get to it."

"Perhaps. But I don't care about them so much as the damage that has been done to the people they married. Maybe the spouses can use it to recoup the money lost from the scholarships. Did Harper ever figure it out?" He told her what she'd told him. "So they went to the bank telling them they had this money coming, and borrowed against it for books and a car. I'm sure they never once thought of buying either."

"Not that Harper could find, no." She hurt for the kids. Her niece and nephew both knew about it now, but it was no less painful for her to know it. "What do you want to do with your money? That is yours too. Your parents did that, especially for you."

"I think I'd like to put it into an account for our children. For them to use for college or a new home. Whatever they need. And I'd like to add to it. You said the money I make from working isn't necessary, so I'm going to bank it, so there is funding should they, or for that matter, anyone, need it for college." She looked at him. "A college fund. For anyone that needs it. Call it the Mary Margaret and LeRoy James Foundation. What do you think?"

"I think that is an amazing idea. I love it. I'm betting the rest of my family will help out with it." Piper loved this man. So very much. "All right, my heart. What do you want to do now?"

"Go back to bed with you." He laughed and picked her up in his arms. "Are you always going to be this easy? If so, we might have to slow down a bit. I'm a little sore from earlier."

"I'll pamper you in the best way possible. Then after that, I will hand feed you dinner, then show you how much I love you with every part of my body." Fisher wiggled his brows at her, and she laughed. "I think, my love, that we have been very remiss in some things. I'm betting I can find a place or two on you that I might have missed earlier. Want me to have a look?"

Piper was positive he'd not missed anything, but she was willing to have him make sure. While he carried her up the stairs, she remembered something that she had in the way of magic. It was to be able to detect when someone was in pain. She wondered how that would come in handy, then was dropped on the bed. Right now, however, she just didn't care.

# Chapter 7

Fisher stood outside the castle doors. His body felt heavy, and looking down at himself, he realized he was in armor. It was a dream. One of long ago, when he had defended such castles for the person with the most coin to be handed over. But this time, he had no army behind him. Looking around, he saw Piper beside him, her manner of dress like his, her hand filled with a sword as big as she was. The comfort it gave him, having her there with him was profound. Looking forward, he saw the great being making his way toward them.

"Where are we?" He didn't understand the question, so he didn't answer her. To give the creature coming toward them any kind of information was something one did not do. "Fisher, are we going to defend the castle?"

"It's our duty." He glanced at her when she told him all right. It was odd, he thought, to have his mate in his dream. But he didn't care. Dreams were safe. "The creature coming to us, it's not human. Can you see that?"

"Troll." He looked around for the voice and saw that Peter and Snowflake were there. "He wants inside. You cannot allow him to breach the gates, my lord. 'Twill be a nightmare should he do that. His army, they are riding horses that are captives. Did you see that? Someone should make sure they aren't harmed."

The dream was different, but only a dream. Telling Snowflake to see if one of the horses could speak to him, she took off toward the others behind the great troll. Once she returned, a white horse, so brilliantly glowing in the morning fog that Fisher had to blink several times in order to see him clearly, returned with her.

"You are a captive of the troll? Would you and the others like to be free?" The horse told him not only were they captives, but they were also shorn of their wings. "Why would he do such a thing to such a creature as yourself?"

*To keep us from flying away, my lord. Can you help us? We will stand with you and your mate, should you need us.* He told him he would be just fine with him and his faeries. However, he said he would set them free to go to their homeland. *You help us, my lord, and we will bow before you to be your servants for life.*

"The queen. She is the one you will bow before." The horse told him he was the one they'd work with. The queen would have to deal with it. Fisher laughed. "I can live with that. This is a dream."

The horse looked at him oddly but said nothing. He took his smaller blade from his sheath and held it tightly in his hand until the gems and stones on it cut deeply into his hand. Once his hand was covered from fingertip to wrist with his own blood, he dropped the blade and put his hand on the snowy nose of the horse. With his other hand, he slammed his sword deep within the soil beneath his feet. The sound of the magic he was using was deafening in its wake.

The sword, a gift from the queen Aurora, was made especially for him. He had no idea when she'd given it to him nor how he knew how it had been made. But in dreams, he knew all sorts of things were easily explained. No other creature or human would ever be able to use his sword. It was light, so it wouldn't tire him using it in a long battle.

The pummel was made from the earth, a gift to him so that he might protect the very thing it was made of from others that might wish to hurt the earth. The blade was made of the finest steel, forged in the greatest fires of the earth's volcanoes. It would never rust, never break so long as it was used for good. When he used the sword, nary a sound would be heard except for the wind, which would allow him to kill his foe before they even realized he was near.

It was a sword made for a warrior, a warrior that would defend the castle he was helping until death. Not his own, but the death of those that dared to try and breach the doors of the castle. Fisher fed the sword with his blood, completing the ritual that would help him win battles.

"I, Lord Fisher Prince, black tiger of the queen Aurora, give you all that was stolen from you. For you and all of your kind." The ground rumbled beneath him, and Fisher had just a moment of worry. Could this be real? But it was a dream. "You will now have my protection so long as you need it."

He removed his bloodied hand and saw the mark that marred the beauty of the white horse. On some level, Fisher knew the mark would be there for all time. It was his mark that claimed the horse as his own.

As soon as his wings appeared on his back, great wings that would be needed to carry such a horse, the horse took to the skies only to return and stand beside Piper. He bowed low before her. Wings opened wide, he looked magnificent—a true beauty in contrast to the blood that would be shed this day.

*I shall be your steed, my lady. You need only to climb upon my back, and I will help you in your fight.* Piper climbed up on the horse and asked him what she should call him. *My name is too hard in your language. So if you'd call me something you like, I shall come to you when you call.*

"What is the meaning of your name?" The horse told Piper what he thought it meant. "Avalanche. It's a good name. You will be called that. The thundering snow coming off a mountainside is the perfect name for one such as yourself."

As Fisher looked out over the field where the troll was standing now, he saw that all that had been riding were now on the ground. Their horses, now with their wings, were flying in the sky, dropping great piles of shit on the top of the soldiers' heads. The very creatures that had shorn their wings before. Fisher laughed so hard he nearly fell onto his sword.

Pulling his sword free of the earth, he held it upright. Snowflake said that Black Knight was here with her men. Asking if she would see him, he wasn't surprised when the faerie, leader and ruler of the great faerie army landed on the pommel of his sword.

"We are ready to serve you, my lord." He nodded. "You need only to say the word, and we will destroy the army before you."

"All but the troll. He needs to be punished by the queen of this castle so that others will think twice about coming here." With one nod, the sky in front of him darkened with the faeries. He was reminded of a murmuration, a great cloud of starlings flying together in a whirling, ever-changing pattern. "Go."

In a matter of seconds, less, he thought, the creatures that had taken up arms with the troll were falling to the ground. Their deaths were quick. They never had the chance to even draw their swords against so many. He moved forward, Piper upon Avalanche beside him, to speak to the troll.

With the tip of his sword, he drew blood from the

creature. The green of its blood ran down along the blade of his weapon as the troll begged for his life. He called him by name, telling him he'd not known such a man as himself was now defending the castle.

"That is your excuse for coming here? You thought it would be easy to take the castle from the queen here?" The troll said his men were hungry. "It looks to me as if you've not pushed away from the table enough, troll. Now that your men are dead, you too will be punished. The queen will tell us what your sentence will be."

"Nay. I will not return if you were to allow me to go. I promise you this on my heart." Piper laughed, and the troll looked at her. "What do you find so funny? You are nothing more than a woman who steals the rides of my men."

Piper slid from Avalanche's back to stand before the creature. He took a step back when she put her hand out to touch him. Fear was palpable from him. When Piper touched only her fingers to his chest, the creature screamed out. Whether from pain or from fear, Fisher didn't know, but when she stepped back, she looked at him.

"The queen said the creatures the troll harmed the most should be the ones to destroy him. His death will not be quick. However, it would satisfy so many for it to be done by the ones he harmed in his pursuit to come here and take the castle." He asked her who that was, and when she looked at Avalanche, he knew. "He and his family. They have suffered the most, Fisher. His mate and their child have been killed to make him bring his team to heel. They have paid the ultimate price."

"All right, then, that is what we'll allow." The troll begged once again as he was lifted into the air by the rest of the horses. Fisher noticed that Avalanche stayed with them. "You have the permission of the queen to do with him as you wish."

*I do. And it means a great deal to me. However, I have pledged myself to your mate, and that alone is payment enough for what he has done to me and my kind.*

Nodding once, Fisher turned away from him. Looking at the castle, he saw Aurora there. Her smile was contagious, and he returned his own back to her. When he was standing before her, she put her hand on his cheek.

"You're not asleep, Fisher. You're here, in my land, defending my castle as you were meant to do." He looked around, then back at her, smiling. "You still do not believe me? When I tell you that you have won a great battle today for all mankind?"

"This is a dream." She shook her head and looked to his right. Piper was there, grinning at him. "It is a dream, right? I mean, I've fought wars such as this before. It's a dream. Tell me I didn't just threaten a troll with nothing more than a sword in my hand."

"You did it quite well if you ask me." Shaking his head, he asked Piper again if she was here in his dream. "No, moron, you're here. With me. If this were a dream, could I hurt you like this?"

The pinch to his nose was painful, but he didn't wake up. Still standing in front of the queen, he rubbed at the pain as he tried to take in what he'd done. Looking back, the dead were being pulled into the earth, their bodies going a long way in helping the earth recover from so much blood.

"I'm here. I'm really here defending your castle. No way." Piper smacked him on the forehead. "I don't understand it. Why do I feel as if I'm dreaming? There has to be a reason for me feeling so confident and strong. Don't you think?"

"You are strong, Fisher. Bigger than your brothers. Stronger than all of them together now. You needed to be, to be there when I call upon you." He looked behind him again as Aurora continued. "What do I have to do to convince you that you've just saved my kingdom?"

He didn't know, but he was no longer sure he'd been dreaming. Fisher looked down at his hand. The wound there was healed, but the scarring, something he'd never had before, was still there—in the shape of a horse. Looking at Avalanche, he realized he had saved him by touching his blood—his blood, not magic—to the forehead of a horse. Fisher dropped to the ground. His legs were trembling hard enough that he was sure everyone could hear his knees knocking together.

"Now, what is upsetting you? Do you need a nap? Or a binky?" He looked up at Piper and thought for sure she was having entirely too much fun at his expense. "Why on earth did you think this was a dream in the first place? I mean, really?"

"How did I get here? I just seemed to wake up here. Also, I don't remember dressing in my armor. Tell me when I did that?" When Piper looked at Aurora, he did as well. "The sword. It was a gift from you. I knew that, but I have no memory of you handing it to me. What would you think if that happened to you?"

"You're right. I would be confused." Aurora snapped her fingers, and they were in the castle. He was dressed in his usual mode of dress—jeans, a T-shirt, and socks. No shoes if he was in the house, which is where he *thought* he had been. "I summoned you. That is how you came here. As for your armor, it is forever on you so that at a moment's notice, such as today, I can call to you, and you won't be hampered by getting dressed. It isn't seen by anyone until you need it. The same with Piper, who is taking this a great deal better than you are, Fisher."

He looked at his mate and pulled her into his lap. The security of having her near him was making him feel less stupid about this entire thing. Fisher told her he was sorry, then did the same to the queen.

"You have no reason to be sorry, Fisher. We won the battle. You were brilliant out there." Piper kissed him on the nose. "Next time we get called out, I'm going to make sure you know you're awake. Or perhaps not. You were very brave, thinking you were asleep. I might keep you that way when a heavy decision needs to be made."

Piper was still giggling when she sat down on the chair again. There was a plate of cookies near her, as well as a tall glass of what looked like orange juice. He took one of her cookies and moaned at the taste.

"They're pineapple crunch cookies. Are they not the best?" Fisher agreed with Aurora as a plate of the same cookies appeared next to him. A glass of the drink too. "That is pineapple orange juice. I saw it in a store once and couldn't get enough of it. So I'm having the cook experiment with different flavors of fruit together. Are you all right now, Fisher?"

"I am. I'm sorry for the way I acted." He still wasn't sure about a couple of things, but let them go. "I don't think it will be that easy again, will it? I mean, the troll was easy to defeat. Will it always be that way, you think?"

"I think for the first time in many years people will think twice about coming here to take my castle. It's important for all creatures, in this land and yours, to be able to come here as a safe haven. Today you took on a troll that has been giving me trouble for a very long time. I think, as I said before, this will make people think twice before they think to take what does not belong to them." Fisher told her he was glad for that. "As am I. You have done me a great service, Fisher and Piper. You will be rewarded nicely."

Before he could tell her that it wasn't necessary, he found himself in his room in bed. Sitting up, he looked around. So it had been a dream, he told himself. Then he looked at his hand. The horse there, the beautiful white Avalanche, winked back at him.

~*~

Louis sat in the chair that had been provided to him and waited. Like he had a choice in the matter. He'd been looking for Mary when a cruiser stopped him from crossing the street and asked him who he was. Lying to them didn't get him anything but cuffed up the side of the head. When he was tossed in the backseat of the cruiser, he was glad the air had been turned all the way up. He'd been sweating like a pig.

Now he was in a building he didn't know, sitting in an office of someone he also didn't know, waiting for someone to tell him what the hell was going on. Louis stood up to pound on the door again when it was opened, and his wife stood there.

"What are you doing here?" She didn't speak but entered the room and sat down. Rachel came in a few seconds later and sat as well. "Are you going to speak to me, Bonny? Or you, Rachel? Are you the reason I was picked up like a common criminal?"

"You're never common anything, Louis. Sit down and shut up." He was surprised by Bonny's tone. She never said a word to him that had any kind of heat to it. But he did sit down when she told him to the second time. "No, I'm not the reason you were brought here. I'm glad they found you, but I didn't do it. Some very wealthy and strong armed people did it."

"So you just hopped in the car and came here because they told you to? I can't even get you to make my favorite dinner. How did they do that?" He was going for a joke, but she glared at him. "Tell me what you know, and perhaps we can get this over with instead of sitting here snipping at each other."

"I was asked, politely, I might add, to come here to finish this with you. A private plane picked me and Rachel up and flew us here yesterday. We were given a nice room at a lovely hotel and then taken to dinner. You've not done that for me in a very long time. Now, I understand why." He asked her why she'd not called him to have him come and stay with her and his daughter. "Because, Louis, you weren't even a thought in my head when they told us you were here with Mary. These people were as kind to us as anyone has ever been, and when they told us what you'd done, divorcing you was a no brainer."

"Divorcing me? No. Why would you want to do that?" She told him what she'd found out. "I have it all figured out. As soon as I get the insurance money from Mom, it'll pay it all off, and we'll be on easy street. You know I'm like a cat. That I'm always landing on my feet."

"This time, you landed yourself into jail. How could you do this to our daughter, Louis? Steal her money? She worked hard in winning that money, and you pissed it away because of one scheme after another. And there is no money from your mother's estate. She was broke. Dead broke, and might well have lived longer had you and that nutball of a sister of yours helped poor Piper out when she asked for it. Your own mother, Louis. You left her to die like she was nothing to you." He started telling her there was money. "No. I've seen what Piper spent of her own money to keep your mother in medications. The list of things they had to do to even make a payment on the funeral was more than they had. The insurance money? The one you've been trying to get? It went for paying for her funeral, and that of your father. You left them with nothing. And that is what you're getting. Nothing."

"Who told you that? Piper? I know for a fact there is—" The paperwork she tossed at him was written in his sister's pen. He knew it was hers too. The girl wrote like there was going to be a grade on anything that she put to paper. "Where did you get this? From her again?"

"The lawyer that came to see us. Not only did he show us every little thing that was purchased, but he also was kind enough to tell us about the money your mother put into an account when you were a child. Enough money, thankfully, to get Rachel and I out of the poor house and pay the back taxes you were supposed to have paid."

"Good old Mom is going to save me." He put out his hand. "Tell me how much it is, Bonny, and I'll make sure it gets into the right hands. You might well have saved me from prison right now. Honey, we're going to be on easy street after this. I'm going to put the money to good use, I promise you."

"I'm not going to give you anything." He told her it

was his. That his mom had saved it. "I don't care if God himself put that money in an account for you. You're not going to need it where you're going. Prison. Right where you belong."

He couldn't believe his wife was speaking to him this way. It was like she was an entirely different person. There was no reasoning with her like this. Louis turned to his daughter, the light of his life right now.

"Don't bother, Father. I'm finished with you too. Had it not been for Aunt Piper, Peter and I would be screwed in being able to go to college. She and her new husband have paid our way into the dorms, as well as given us each enough money to pay our tuition and books for the next four years. Longer if we need it." Louis told her that was why he needed the money, he wanted to put her on easy street too. "Sure, you do. I was already on easy street, as you call it, but you fucked that up for me when you decided my education wasn't as important to you as the next deal. As I said, I'm done with you. Don't expect me to feel sorry for you or to help you in any way. You're a terrible father, and always have been."

"That's not fair. How did you come up with me not being a good father to you?" She sent her own paper toward him. On it was a list of money that he'd *borrowed* from her. Birthday money, Christmases when they'd been so broke they couldn't even have a nice meal. There were a lot of them too. "This is what a family does, Rachel. They support each other and their dreams."

"My dream was for you to pay me back when you took my money. My dream was for me to go to college to become a good attorney so that I could see you put in prison for the way you treated us. Not to mention how you treated Grandma and Grandpa. They were so ill, and you left them to die. Aunt Piper is the only one in your family that never gave up on them." Rachel stood up. "I will see you in hell before I have anything to do with you again. You have taken and taken my entire life, and I'm finished with having to watch as you destroy Mom too."

He looked at his wife when Rachel left them there. She was crying, and he didn't understand what she had to be so upset about. Rachel had yelled at him, not her. He finally couldn't take it anymore and slammed his hands on the table.

"Straighten up and wipe those tears away. What is going on here? Why am I the bad guy in all this?" Louis shook his head. "You had a roof over your head, didn't you? A car to drive around. All that was because of me."

"I had a job that I didn't tell you about. I worked every day at a shit job so we could eat and have a car to drive." He asked her why she'd had to hide it from him. That he could have used that money. "Because you would have taken it. The very food from our mouths to feed this insane idea you have that scamming people is the only way to make it. Well, it's not. Do you have any idea how many times I've had a bill collector come by the house to shut off something? Weekly. It was always about you, Louis. About the next big scam. The one that was going to make you rich. Would it have ever been enough, had you followed through on any of them?"

"There are people like me all over the world, making money at some of the things I was trying. I just don't understand why you felt you had to have all the money you made. You didn't treat me well, Bonny. I hope you understand that. I'm ashamed to call you my partner in life for not giving me money when I needed it." She stood up. "Where are you going? I don't have a pot to piss in here. You'll have to give it to me now, or I'll be living on the streets. You don't want that, do you? I'm your husband."

"You were my husband, Louis. I filed for divorce and was granted it when the judge heard what sort of person you are. As for you living on the streets? I want you to think about what would have happened to me and your daughter had I not gotten my ass out there and gotten a job. Would it have been all right for us to have been in the same predicament?" He told her it wasn't the same. "Of course you'd say that, wouldn't you? It's all about you."

When she left him there, he decided to go and get her. She had to have some money on her. Enough for him to fund an idea he had in his head. Before he could get to the door, a well dressed man and three officers came into the room with him. He was told to sit and to shut up for the second time today.

"Now see here. I don't know what's going on here, but my wife and I need to finish our conversation. She's trying to take the money that my mom left me." The man in the suit introduced himself as Federal Agent Mick Banks. "So? I don't care who you are. I have things to do."

"I'm afraid you're not going to be able to do that, Mr. James. You're under arrest." He was read his rights then told what he was being taken in for. The list was longer than he thought it should be. When cuffs were put on him, the agent spoke again. "You're going to be taken to the jail for the next several days, then you will be moved back to Nevada where you're going to be facing charges. Do you have any questions?"

"I have plenty. What's the bail going to be? You'll have to go find my wife. She's taken all my money. Whatever it is, you tell her she has to pay it. I don't want to go to prison anywhere." The cops laughed, and he tried to think what they might have thought was so funny. As he was being dragged to the elevator, he saw his sister, Mary. "They're arresting me, Mary. You have to do something. I don't want to go to prison. Bonny took all my money. You need to see if —"

"What the hell do you expect me to do for you, Louis? In the event you didn't notice, I'm being arrested too. My own husband called the cops on me. My own fucking husband did this." She struggled with the police for a moment before she turned back to him. "Yeah, I had some money too, but it's going to Paddy. For his hardship of being married to me. I'm going to show him what hardship is as soon as I'm out of here."

He was shoved into an elevator before he could talk to his sister any more. Once the doors opened, he was taken to another room and told to behave. Like he was five years old or something. Mary was brought in a few minutes later, but whenever he started to talk to her, he was told to keep his mouth shut. What was wrong with people today? No one seemed to have the slightest bit of manners.

"What are we doing in here? Do you have another revelation to tell us about money that we can't have? Have you, by chance, figured out that we're the victims in all this? That we've been screwed over by our own flipping family? This is bullshit." He watched as the door opened and a man walked in straightening his tie. "What is he going to tell us? That we're aliens from a different world, and we're screwed?"

"My name is Fisher Prince." An incredibly beautiful woman came in and sat down. He didn't know who she was, but Louis wanted to get to know her. "Hey, moron. That's your sister. My wife."

Louis looked at the woman, then back at the man. When he nodded, Louis stared hard at the woman. Jesus H. Christ, she looked just like their mother had when she was younger. Except for the white streak of hair, she could have been her double. Then it occurred to him what the man had said.

"You're married to Piper? Do you have any idea what sort of person she is?" Fisher looked at Piper. Jealousy ran over Louis's body. He'd never felt that before, the feeling of being jealous of how a man looked at a woman. Louis didn't think he'd ever had that look when staring at his wife. "You actually love her, don't you?"

"I do. More with every beat of my heart." Louis's body took another jolt then. He'd never said those kinds of words to his wife. Not even his child. But this man said it freely. Louis would bet he meant every word of it too. "We're here to tell you we've taken care of your children. They'll be going to college as they should have been."

As he droned on about what his and Mary's family was going to get, Louis thought of his own life. What he'd gotten out of it. It occurred to him he had nothing to show for being on this earth for the last forty or so years. Even his home had been taken from him, according to the paperwork Bonny had left him. His daughter had also written him off. Not that it mattered, he supposed. He'd gotten himself into this mess, he was going to get himself out. He looked at the man when he realized he was no longer speaking.

"Boy, do I have an investment for you, buddy. Now that we're family, I can even give you the family discount." Fisher picked up his paperwork, and he and Piper walked out of the room. "You need time to think about it. That's all right. I'll talk to you later."

When they put him in the back of a cruiser to take him who knew where, he thought of all the things he could do now that he realized Piper had money. As soon as they were wherever they were going, he was going to make sure he wrote all his new ideas down. Yes, he thought, he'd be out of this crap by the end of the week for sure.

# Chapter 8

Piper made her way to the jail. She'd been summoned, for lack of a better term, by both Mary and Louis. Somehow they had tracked her to Ohio. She didn't have any idea what they might want, but here she was to find out. Their lives had really turned to shit, it seemed to her. Having nothing to do with what got them here, she wasn't upset to be demanded to come here.

The jail was a small town place. She knew in the morning, they would both be taken back to their home state. While she knew they'd both be going to jail, what sort of time they'd spend there wasn't anything that she concerned herself with.

She sat down at the table she'd been led to. Looking around, she was charmed by the place. Piper doubted there were many small town jails left. There would be none like this one. It reminded her of the one that had been on television a long time ago. Her mom and dad had watched the repeats every evening when she'd been living at home.

The room she was in, a medium sized open room, had several tables around just like the one she was at, windows with curtains on them, and plants sitting on the sills. An old fashioned pop machine worked on the honor system. You paid for your drink from the big fridge by putting the money in the empty can on the top. The chairs were a mismatched bunch, comfortable but sturdy.

She saw Mary and Louis coming toward her. Louis was limping for some reason, but Mary was talking a mile a minute to the person with her. They were both in chains, wrists and ankles, but neither of them seemed to be talking to each other. She wondered at that until they sat down.

"Why is he here?" Piper didn't answer Mary because she didn't know the answer. Looking at the guard who had brought her here, she put to him the same question. "He's a bad influence. I don't want to be seen associating with him anymore."

"You either do this now, Mary, or you go back to your cell until tomorrow. Your sister has come all the way here to talk to you at your request, so talk or not. It's up to you." The trip had taken her only fifteen minutes because she'd walked. Smiling to herself, Piper looked at Louis.

"Did you want something from me, Louis?" He looked at her, and she smiled. At that moment, he looked like the teenager she remembered when they were still living at home. "Louis, you wanted to speak to me. What is it you want me to do for you before you leave?"

"Did you know about the money?" She said she'd been the one to find it. "Then why did you make sure that Bonny knew about it? Mom put that away for me to have. Not my wife. I was going to invest it in things that might well have gotten me out of here."

"I doubt that any amount of money would have gotten you out of here, Louis. You're being sentenced on mail fraud. That's a serious crime. Not to mention, you took all those people's money and didn't have it to return to them." He said it was his money that Mom had wanted him to have. "I understand that. But your family is in need of it more than you're going to be where you're going. Just chalk it up to, since you didn't know about it, they have a nice nest egg to start over with."

He turned his back to her as well as he could, she supposed, being in chains.

Piper looked at Mary. Mary was glaring at her as if she'd done something terribly wrong, when in fact, Piper had had nothing at all to do with either of them being arrested or held.

"You have money, don't you?" She nodded, not really wanting to get into any kind of discussion about how much money Fisher told her they both had now. "I don't understand how you turned out to be the one with all the money, and Louis and I are ruined. You should have just given us what we wanted, and we wouldn't be here. It's not fair. You understand that, don't you?"

"I'm not sure what you mean by saying it's not fair. I

met and fell in love with someone who just happened to have money. He's a wonderful person. I'd like to have you meet him sometime." Mary told her no. "Suit yourself. But you're not going to drag me down with you in this. You've made your bed, and now you're going to have to learn to lie in it."

"That's easy for you to say, sitting there in your beautiful clothes and your hair all pretty. While I'm sitting here in a jumpsuit that has been worn by god only knows how many other people, and awaiting trial for trying to get something that should have been mine in the first place." Piper asked her if she meant the money. "Of course, I mean the money. Don't be obtuse. Money is what makes the world go around. I don't have any, so I'm stuck here. I want you to try and get me a good attorney. Paddy told me I'm on my own. He actually filed for divorce."

"I would have too had I been married to you. You nearly made him lose his company by taking what you did from it. Have you no shame for even taking Peter's scholarship from him?" Mary told her it wasn't any of her business. "No, I guess it's not. None of this is. But you asked to see me, and here I am. If all you wanted to do was to rehash the things you both did to put yourself here, then I'm going to go."

"Will you come and see us?" Louis was still turned from her when he asked. She asked him to look at her. "I'm fine the way I am. I asked if you'd come see me. While I'm in jail. My daughter won't. I don't care if Bonny does or not. She took my money, but it hurts me that Rachel wrote me off. Will you come and see me while I'm in prison? Bring me things if I can have them?"

"I will. I don't know how often, but yes, I'll come and see you if you want." He nodded. "What sort of things would you like me to bring you, Louis? I realize I haven't any idea what your likes or dislikes are anymore."

"I like to read—the classics. I used to have a whole collection of them that I would read over and over. They're from a time I thought was prim and proper." He looked at her then. "We did you wrong. I know that now. I've been doing a lot of thinking while here. We should have given you a break or two. At least come to see Mom. She was a good mom. We couldn't have done better if we'd got to pick her out for us. About the books, I had a reader, but I'm betting that Bonny threw it out when she did me."

She didn't say anything to him. As she'd told him, she didn't know him well and didn't know if he was baiting her or not. Writing down to ask Bonny for the reader, she made another note to see if he could have one when he went to prison. Piper asked Mary if she wanted anything.

"Other than getting out of here, I can't think of a single thing." Mary turned to look around the now empty room. "I'd like for you to come and see me too. If you've a mind to, that is. Also, I really like to read too. When we was growing up, before you were born, Dad used to read to us every night. Not that him stopping had anything to do with you. He just stopped, I guess. I think it was because we'd both learned how to read on our own. I'd also like to have you bring me some pictures. Pretty ones. Flowers and stuff. I don't imagine I'll get much of a chance to see them where I'm going."

"I'll check to see if you can have a plant. Would you like that?" Mary nodded and said she liked pansies. "I do, as well. They're happy looking. I put some on Mom's grave, along with carnations on Dad's when I was there last."

Mary looked at her then. There was a sadness to her eyes like she was coming to terms with something and didn't care for the outcome of it. Without a thought to the rules, Piper reached for her sister's hand and held it. Mary leaned her head on it and sobbed hard about how much of a fool she'd been.

The guard didn't say anything to either of them. When Louis took her other hand, he held it to his cheek as he too cried. Overwhelmed with emotions, Piper felt her own tears fall over her cheeks. She had not expected this in coming here today. It wasn't something she would have thought she wanted either. But she did. Piper needed it too.

When they pulled away, she did as well, wiping at her tears so they'd not say something to ruin what they'd just shared. She asked them if there was anything else she could get for them when Louis nodded.

"Do you have any pictures of you? Also, some of Mom and Dad? I'd like a couple of them if you'd not mind. I don't know the rules on such things, but I'd like to talk to the pictures every once in a while. Talk to Mom and Dad and tell them what an imbecile I'd been." Piper wrote it down, hiding the tears that fell again. "Also, if it would be all right, maybe you could bring your husband next time. I mean, just if he'd like to come see us. I know I'd like to get to know him better. I promise you, I won't talk about having him give me money for any more of my projects."

By the time she'd been told her time was up, she had a list of things that she would bring them the next time she saw them. Her heart was so full she nearly didn't ask on her way out if some of the things on the list could be taken to them. The lady at the desk was so sweet, she handed her a box of tissues as she went over the list.

"These things might be all right, I'm guessing. But they'll also be things that could be stolen. Like that reader thing, you have on here. You'd be better off bringing books. There aren't too many in prison that would read a classic. I'm not saying they won't, but your brother might stand a better chance of keeping books than he would a reader." Piper marked that off her list. "You could also bring them things they could trade with. I don't know a lot about prison life, mind you, but there are things they might not be able to get without some help. Also, there is a commissary. There is an account for everyone that people put money in for them to get things they won't be given— mostly personal things like deodorant and mouthwash. Also, letters and such. That can make them feel more connected to you and the ones they won't be able to see."

"How much money do you think they'd need?" She told her. "All right. I can do that. I'll set that up with my husband so they can have a couple of hundred dollars a month in it. I guess they'd be using it for things they don't usually get given to them."

"That's right. Luxury items mostly. Candy if they wish. You could give them a nice warmer blanket—put their names on them. Comb, toothpaste, and such. A razor too, for both males and females. Pen and paper as well. When my uncle was in prison a very long time ago, he wanted pretty paper to write to his wife. He also sprayed some of his cologne on it. I don't know why I've told you that, but there you have it."

Armed with her list of things she could make sure they had now, she went to the local store to pick things up. She didn't know many of the townspeople, but they seemed to know who she was. Fisher, apparently, was friends with just about all the town. Then Buck joined her as she was looking at the blankets for her brother and sister. She told him what she was doing here.

"That's not going to be something they might need out in Nevada where they're going to be spending time, do you think? The blankets, I mean." Piper told Buck she'd not thought of that. "I mean, you should get them one. Just on the off chance, they might need a snuggle or two. Here, honey, let me help you with your brother's things. That razor you have there, it's not fit for a man unless pulling out his beard is what you want."

With Buck's help, she was able to get just what she needed. He made suggestions on several of the things she was getting for her sister too. He told her to buy the large candy bars so the treat would last longer. She knew then that he had a sweet tooth for all things sweet.

"How about you have dinner with this old man?" Piper laughed and told him he could pass for a brother to his sons. "Yes, well, that's the thing about being immortal. You don't age past a certain time in your life. You'll see it too as the years go by. I'm an old man. I have no problem with that. But if I was a sickly man, I might be upset about having to be sick and old too."

Telling Fisher what she was up to, he asked if he could join them. Buck was excited to have just the two of them to himself and agreed. However, it turned out to be a large family reunion as more and more of the Prince family came by to grab a bite too.

Piper loved this family. They were loud and loved to argue. Mostly she could understand what was going on but really didn't care what the conversation was about. So long as they were good natured about it, she laughed right along with them. Sara sat down next to her.

"I wanted to thank you for hanging out with Buck today. He was feeling sorry for himself." Piper asked her what had happened. "Nothing. Not really. He just was feeling down, and I was a little busy when he wanted me to coddle him. He doesn't need it often, but today he did."

"Is there anything he needs? Besides a kick in the butt?" Sara laughed and told her she thought he needed something to do. "A job? I can help him with that. Yes, I think I might have the perfect job for him."

~*~

Fisher loved seeing Piper and his dad get their heads together. It had only been one day since she'd asked Dad for his help, and the two of them were making great strides in getting the supplies they needed to take to prisons.

"You see? Right there is what I'm talking about." He looked at what Dad was talking about as he pointed to the computer. "The more you buy, the bigger discount you can get. Not as big as I'd like, mind you, but we can put the rest of what we get into storage. Maybe we can get the faeries to build us something bigger."

"No." Both he and Piper answered Dad at the same time. "Dad, if you get them to build you something bigger, you might not be able to walk from one end of it to the other. You should see Piper's camper. I swear to you, they must have been on some sort of catnip or something when they were 'enlarging' it for her."

"What do you mean?" He nodded and asked Dad to come with him. Piper was still laughing as they made their way out to the camper, which was serving as her computer office. Dad walked in first. "Oh my. Yes, oh, my goodness. You'd never tell it was this big from the outside, would you?"

Not only was there a very large working area, but the

bedroom she'd had in here was as big if not bigger than the one they slept in. The bathroom had a sauna, a shower, as well as a double sink and tub. The kitchen had a double refrigerator, a dishwasher, and a table big enough to serve twelve people. Dad was laughing as he looked at the monster-sized television that took up one entire wall.

"I have five computers here too." Piper showed Dad the computers and the monitors that were in the room. The camper had only been twenty-four feet long when it was brought here. But now it was large enough on the inside, with four bedrooms, three bathrooms, and a playroom, to have a family of five living there. "They've come in handy, I won't lie about that, but it's just too much for one person to work in out here. I thought we might just have someone live out here that works for us instead of me working here. I've not done it yet because I didn't want to hurt their feelings. They're very proud of what they've done for me."

"Yes, I can see where having them do something like this would be a bit overwhelming." Dad opened up the fridge and handed them each a bottle of cold water. "I'm betting there isn't an electrical outlet anywhere in here, is there? This whole thing, it's running on magic."

"I did ask them about that, as well as the Internet. They told me that no one would ever be able to trace anything about my computers because it's a special connection. I didn't ask what that meant." They looked around for a few more minutes, laughing at some of the things that were put in. "Do you suppose they think this is larger than life, or that they're tinier for the size? That sounded so much better in my head."

Laughing again, they made their way back to the house. Dad was ticking off things that he needed to take care of but wasn't going to worry over. Dad and Piper went back to the dining room table where they'd been working, and Fisher made his way to his office. There were things he had to do to get ready for later tonight.

The police had come by earlier this morning and asked him to help them find a lost child. He had expected them to be over several hours ago, but they called and told him they'd be around about four. It was going on three now. He didn't know what they were expecting with this, but he had to mentally prepare himself for what he might find when looking for children.

Two years ago, almost to the day, he'd been asked to look for someone lost. It was an older gentleman that had supposedly walked out of a nursing home. He didn't have any family around—most of his children and grandchildren had stopped visiting him long ago. Fisher had felt sorry for the old man.

A nurse, one that had taken care of Mr. Johnson for a few years, was beside herself with worry. When Fisher had shown up at the nursing home to help out, he found the nurse in Mr. Johnson's room sitting on the big bed. He asked her if there had been any word.

"No, not yet, but I have a feeling you're not going to find him alive and kicking. His grandson called just before you got here and asked if they could have a refund on his room. It's not even been around yet that he's missing." Fisher picked up the man's shirt that was still lying on the floor. "He's a good man. Cranky at times, but I think it's just from being lonely."

As soon as he touched the shirt, he knew not only where the man was but that he'd been murdered. It wasn't his family that had done it either. It was the woman staring at him from the bed.

"Do you want to tell me what happened?" She shook her head and laid back down on the pillow that was on the unmade bed. "I've contacted the police to let them know, as I was asked to do. They're on their way here."

"He could be really cranky when he had his mind set on something. I didn't mean to overdose him, but he was getting on my last nerve yesterday. Demanding things and calling me stupid. He's never done that before." Fisher had contacted his brother as soon as he knew the circumstances surrounding the death of Mr. Johnson. Kylan had contacted the police and told them what he'd been able to share with him. "I just wanted him to be quiet for five minutes. But he wanted to be read to, and I just didn't have it in me. So I just gave him a little more of his sleep meds to put him out. I didn't know he'd been not taking them. He didn't like being drugged up when the sun went down, he told me. So when I gave him just a little too much, to keep him quiet, it was too much for his system all at one time. He should have been taking his medication, and he'd not be dead."

"I've called the police, as I told you. You're going to have to go downtown with them to explain what happened." She shook her head at him. "I'm sorry about this. I truly am. Why did you call me to find him if you didn't want to go to jail?"

"I wanted someone to tell the police what I'd done." He'd been confused about her answer until she pulled a gun from under the pillow. "Tell his family I'm sorry."

Fisher didn't reach her in time to stop her. As soon as the gun was at her chin, she pulled the trigger. He was still sitting there when the police arrived, blood and other things he didn't want to think about all over the wall behind the bed. It was one of the worst jobs he'd ever helped with. Since then and well before.

The police arrived at his home just as the front clock was chiming the hour. When they sat in the chairs in front of his desk, Franklin, a cop from way back, put a baggie on his desk. He didn't say anything, but his partner had plenty to say.

"We think the child is in the septic tank in the back of their property. They said they don't know where he is, but I think they're lying." Fisher asked him why he thought that. "Just my gut feelings. I'm new to being a cop, but I know a lot about human nature."

Fisher glanced at his partner, who was still quiet. Not wanting any more information from newbie, Fisher touched the little dolly and looked at the cop. Fisher was ready to hand the kid his ass when the older man spoke.

"I have a feeling he's still out there. That someone took the little tyke and is loving him to pieces right about now. I don't know if that's what I want you to tell me, but I think my version is a great deal less horrific than the story the man sitting here next to me has painted." The kid snorted. Fisher put the doll back in the bag and handed it to the older man. "He alive?"

"Yes. He was with his grandma, who took him out of his crib earlier this morning and wandered off with him. She has been living with her son and his family since it was apparent that she wasn't able to care for herself." The older cop asked him where he was now. The grandma wasn't missing. "No. I'd say she made her way back to the house on her own but had forgotten where she stashed the little boy. She's hidden him away from the Germans. You'll find that she was a child during the holocaust and still remembers hiding from them."

Nodding, he thanked him for his help. Fisher looked at the younger man, who was saying she should have been put in a place where she was safe. Behind locked doors, so she'd not be wasting their time with shit like this, not able to roam around like everyone else. He told Fisher that anyone over the age of seventy should have monitors put in their heads so they could be tracked easier too.

Fisher shook his head and looked at the boy. "You have no idea what that woman, as a child, went through trying to survive what was done to her. The things that she had to do to survive. How she found food when there wasn't anything around." Fisher stood up. "You know shit about human nature. That woman had only one thought in her head about keeping her grandson safe, and she did it. Now, if you don't mind getting your fucking ass out of my house, I'd be grateful."

"Sheesh, who shit in your oatmeal?" Fisher took a step toward the kid, and he put his hand on the gun. "Touch me, and I'll kill you. I'm not some snot-nosed kid to be fucking with, mister."

Sitting back at his desk, Fisher picked up his phone and called the station house where these two were from. It was nothing for him to ask to speak to the commanding officer of the place by name. Fisher, after all, had been around a very long time.

After telling him how he'd been spoken to and what the younger man had said to him, the CO, Butch Ardell, said he'd be there in ten minutes. Cory Wayne, the younger cop, was told to sit still and to not leave before his boss arrived. Officer Sherman left to go and get the little boy.

"You didn't have to call my boss, you know. If you didn't like what I was saying, then you should have said something." Fisher told him he had done something. He'd called for his boss. "I'm going to get into trouble over this. I hope you're happy about that."

"Actually, I'm thrilled to death knowing that. It would please me even more if you were to lose your job. I can't imagine the things you might have said to the parents of this boy or his grandma." Cory said he was vocal when he saw something wrong. "Yes, but in this case, you couldn't have been more wrong about what happened. Leaping to judgments without all the information is not the way to be a good cop. As I said, I hope you lose your job."

When Butch arrived, he asked to speak to Cory alone. Leaving them in his office, Fisher went to find his wife and dad. Right at that moment, he needed to be around good people, and nothing like the one he'd just left. When Cory and Butch left, Cory was in cuffs and his gun, Fisher was told, was in his office. The stupid kid had pulled his gun on his CO. What a strange world they lived in, Fisher thought.

Hugging his dad first, he sat down next to Piper while she made decisions on what sort of boxes they needed to make their prison care packages. Dad was on the phone, talking to someone about how to get the boxes inspected before they were sent in. This was one of the better projects he was going to get to be a part of. He'd bet that before it was all done, his entire family would be looking into a way to help out.

# Chapter 9

Kylan woke from a deep sleep. While he didn't know what was going on, he knew someone needed him, or what he could do for them. Waiting just long enough for the creature to reach out to him again, he spoke to the tiger as he pulled himself from bed and headed to the shower.

*Do you know where you are*? The cat, a tiger, said it was always warm. She thought she was in a place called California. *I know where that is. Are you in a zoo? A place with other animals*?

*Yes.* He could almost taste her pain. *I'm to have cubs soon. Tomorrow, I think. They told me you could help me. To make it so I'd be safe.*

*Who*? He paused in brushing this teeth and waited for her answer. When it came, he was both relieved and happy that she had someone she could trust. *The faeries all know us. If she recommended us to you, then you'll be all right.*

*I was held captive in a human home, to be brought out to*

*show other humans that I was his prize. They bred me, then took away my children before I could even suckle them. If this place takes them away too, I shall die.* He told her he was on his way. *You are the black tigers that have spread your magic around, are you not?*

*I'm one of them, yes.* He was racing down the stairs when he had a thought. *What makes you think you're going to lose your children? Have you heard them say something?*

*Nay, my lord. I have heard them talking about my babes, but nothing more than that I am too old to breed again. I know not what that means, but I could have babes so long as they need me to.* Kylan made his way to the airport, so happy that as a family, they had the means for him to just go when it was necessary. By the time he got to the airport, the flight manifest was already finished up, and he was on the way. *I'll be there very soon. I'm going to have someone fix it so I can see you as soon as I arrive. I'm going to do everything I can to make sure you get to keep your babes.*

He understood why she thought they'd take her babies from her. Past experience, he knew, could really sour a person or animal to all sorts of things. He himself hated to be in closed rooms. It would make him have a panic attack faster than anything else. Kylan knew why too.

Once, when he'd been about five or six years old, he'd gone into an abandoned house. It hadn't been far from their home, but he was alone, something they'd been warned not to do by not only their parents but by the queen herself. But he'd gone into it, trying, he knew now, to prove he wasn't afraid, when all along, he was shaking so badly that his knees hurt for days after.

The house had no roof to speak of. It had long since been removed for the slate to repair some other home, he was sure. There was enough of it left that the one room off the kitchen was dark with shadows and spider webs. It was the smell that drew him in. It wasn't pleasant by any means, but it was something he'd never smelled before, so he went into it to investigate.

The door to the room was missing. If it had been still hanging there, he might not have felt so safe about entering the room. But almost as soon as he was within the room, the wall behind him collapsed, and the room he was in was shut completely off. Kylan was left in darkness so black he couldn't see his own hand, even holding it up to touch his nose.

Kylan didn't want to panic. Breathing in his nose and out his mouth, as he'd been told to do when he'd had a splinter removed by his mom, wasn't helping like it had before. Even moving to stand close to the wall didn't help. The thing was slick with something oozing, and his mind, already on high alert, went off the wire, and he couldn't catch his breath.

*Stop breathing like that.* He swallowed in a mouth full of air when he heard from his brother Fisher. *You're going to pass out, and I won't be able to find you. Where are you, anyway?*

*In the old house at the back of the property.* Fisher asked him if he was stupid. *Not that I know of. But coming in here,*

*I sure do feel like it. Are you coming?*

*I am. What made you think you could be brave enough to go into that thing anyway? Isn't the floor like nothing but dust?* It occurred to him later, much later, that Fisher was talking to him to keep him calm. *I'd think the no trespassing signs would have been a first giveaway on how you're not supposed to enter. You sure can be dumb when you want to be, can't you, Kylan?*

He talked to him, making fun of him and teasing him about his choices. Bad ones anyway. By the time he saw a little light coming from above, Kylan was more upset at Fisher than he was scared. As soon as Fisher had an opening for him to get out of, he leapt at his brother and tussled with him until they were both laughing so hard they had to rest.

To this day, he knew Fisher had never told any of the others, especially their parents. When they arrived home, dirty and dusty, Mom only made them clean up outside instead of messing up her clean floor. Kylan knew for that reason alone, and so many other times Fisher had come to his aid on one thing or another, that Fisher was his best friend as well as brother. He'd saved him. Not his life perhaps, but he'd saved him all the same.

The plane landed at a little after four in the morning. There was an envelope for him at the ticket counter that held his badge, telling anyone who read it he was a veterinarian—one who specialized in tigers. He also had an appointment at eight with the head of the feline department of the zoo, as well as hotel reservations and a car to rent. Having people in place for this sort of thing, faeries in the human world, made this sort of job much easier than it was before travel was so easy.

The zoo, of course, wasn't open to the public, but he was let in by showing them his badge. According to the paperwork he had been given, he was there to look over the cages of the tiger display, as well as to check on one or two of the big cats. Normal procedure. He was taken to the birthing suite almost as soon as he was taken to the cat area.

"She's been in labor for a couple of days. I don't think she wants to birth them." Kylan asked the man, Arnold, why he thought that. "We've only had her here for a few weeks. The people that owned her before were keeping her in a cage and breeding her for the cash. It took the police about six months to close this case. The cat was already breeding when we got her. She's older than most cats we have, but almost feral when it comes to having exams and stuff."

"You said she was bred, correct?" Arnold said they'd sell off her cubs for the money without her even getting to be around them. "Well, I'm not sure, but I'm betting she's terrified you're going to be doing the same thing to her. She might just be protecting her babies before they're taken from her."

"You think so?" He knew so but didn't tell him how he knew. She'd told him that. "We all have been calling her

Ginger. If she had a name with the other folks, we didn't get it. I'm betting you're right about her being afraid. Ginger never acted out like she is now until we brought her in for an exam this time. Yes, sir, I think you're right on the nose with that."

He moved slowly toward the cat and let her smell that he was one as well. Kylan was worried that him being a male might upset her, so he spoke to her through their link and told her who he was. She not only accepted him right away, but Ginger also purred.

Examining her was easy. He knew more about her through their link than any of the equipment he was free to use would have told him. While no one was looking at him, he gave her magic to make one of her cubs into a black tiger. Kylan gave her an extra boost and hoped that two of the four she was having would be black tigers. It was the least he could do for a tiger that had suffered so much at the hand of humans.

Almost as if she sensed she was going to be all right, Ginger went into hard labor. The first cub born was a golden one. It was beautiful to look at, and Ginger cleaned her up as soon as she was put back to her body.

The second cub, also a female, was born golden. Kylan was so happy he wanted to take them all home with him and raise them with Ginger. The momma was doing just fine too. Her natural instincts kicked in right away, and she made sure they were both warm and snuggled close to her.

When the third cub came out, the fourth one was right behind him. The two black tigers drew a lot of attention from the people around Ginger. She thanked Kylan several times as he helped with the clean up around her. Her paw on his arm was comforting to him, but he also knew it might well alarm the others around him.

*You've given me such a great gift, my lord.* He said it was his pleasure to do so. *Will they take them from me now? I cannot bear being parted from them after having them so close to me.*

*I'm to understand you'll remain in this room with them for the next few days. After that, you and your cubs will be put in a holding area so you can show off your children to the public. There will be a great many humans here to see such a rare thing as the blacks.* Ginger thanked him several times as the cubs were weighed and measured for the records. *They're trying to figure out names for them. Is there anything you'd like to have one of them called? Because I was here, they're allowing me to name one of them.*

*Sultan.* He loved the name and asked if they could call one of the black tigers the name. They, too, thought it was a perfect name for one of them. *You have done so much for me, my lord — more than I ever expected when I was told to reach out to you. I have my babies here with me. My black tigers too. Thank you from the bottom of my heart.*

Kylan spent the day at the zoo. It was a lovely place. The animals seemed to be well cared for. He spent some time with Arnold and was glad for that. He was a good man and would do just about anything for the cats he was in charge of. When it was time for him to leave, Kylan did something he rarely did. He gave the other man not only his email address so that he could send him pictures of the cats, but also his cell number in the event there was a problem.

Staying at the hotel for the night, he treated himself to a nice dinner before going to bed. Even with the time difference, he was ready to go to bed on his hours. Lying on the bed, thinking about the times he'd done this very thing, helped out tigers by making them somewhat famous, he wondered if it would be a job for him to do for the rest of his days. It was something he enjoyed over any other job he'd done over the years. He told Fisher what he'd been up to.

*We've never had two black cubs born at the same time. Why this time?* He explained to his brother what had happened to Ginger before being taken to the zoo. *You did right then. She needed something to make her special. And that was perfect. The fact that they might never know who the father was or his lineage will make it all the more special. They'll be looking for years on how this happened. Not to mention the zoo getting more visitors.*

*They have this camera set up so people can keep an eye on the cubs and mom all the time. They'd done it for the local schools, but now everyone is pulling it up to watch. With them having two black cubs, it might break the Internet.* They both laughed. *I was going to ask you to go with me, but I figured with you having a mate now, you'd be too busy.*

I would have gone too. *Piper is working on a code for a business. She's already gone to the company and told them about their Internet use. I think she told me more than half the time spent on the computers is not work related. She's going to have to cut that in half.* Kylan asked him why he seemed like she didn't want to do it. *The company shows a great deal of profit. The work that comes from their employees is great. She's afraid if they can't fool around on the computer when they want, that production will go down, and people won't be as gung ho about working for some kind of fun sucker.*

*She might be right. I know a few people that work from home. They also have their games set up so that when they want, they can just pop over and play a round of poker or something along those lines. Terry told me he's getting far more work done in a day because he has an outlet when he needs a break. I guess when he was working in an office, like this company, they took his fun away. Their profit margin dropped by several points the very next day.* Fisher said he'd tell Piper that when she came back in. *How's it working out with the queen? I have to tell you; I might well have been the same way about it being a dream. Someone might have mentioned that to you when you got the position.*

*It's all right. We've had to go there once more, but not to defend the castle. Aurora gifted us some gems to have broken down and sold off.* Kylan asked him what his plans for the gems were. *We've started this huge undertaking, giving care packages to some of the people in prison. It's not much, not really, but the first bunch we sent out were well received. It's a couple of books and some sweets. Also some socks and a voucher for the commissary. I think it's about twenty bucks. Enough, I was told, to get them a few things they might want. It's something Piper is very focused on, and it's been a great deal of fun for the faeries. They're loading the boxes with the things we get in. She and Dad are working on some ways to get some donations of things.*

*Sounds like she's getting some things done. How do you feel about this?* Fisher laughed. *You miss her, don't you? I can tell by your tone that you miss the hell out of having her all to yourself.*

*That's it exactly. But I also know this is going to help a great many people. They've done wrong, don't get me wrong about that. However, I also think that sometimes just having a little something like a candy bar can make your day go from shitty to not so bad. And in prison, I would imagine every day is shitty.* Kylan agreed with him. *If you get home in time, come over for dinner. I don't have a clue what we're having, but it'll be fun having you around. You can tell Piper about the newborns. You have pictures, I'm betting.*

*I do, as a matter of fact. Also, she can watch them grow on the Internet.* They were both laughing. *I'm wide awake now, so I think I'll see about coming home now. Sleeping in my own bed sounds a lot better than staying here for no other reason.*

Kylan was home by eight-thirty and went to his bed. Falling onto it, he didn't even bother with blankets or the pillow. Willing his clothing away, Kylan was asleep almost as soon as his head hit the pillow.

~*~

Benson waited for someone to let him into his home. He'd been doing a great deal of soul searching the last few days, mostly about himself and what a monumental prick he was. There wasn't any doubt about it either. Working for him must have been a nightmare. Even doing business with him hadn't been any better, he'd bet.

"Sir?" He told Billy, their butler, that Denise had asked him to come over. "Yes sir, she told us, but you're not wearing a suit?"

"I'm not." Benson laughed a little bit. "I guess I never realized how uncomfortable I'd been all these years. I enjoy this new look for me. What do you think?"

"You look relaxed." Billy flushed a bright red. "I'm sorry, sir. I shouldn't have said that. It was unprofessional of me."

"It was honest, and I'm happy to hear it. Thank you." He came into the house and noticed that Denise had been busy. "She's keeping you on your toes, I can see. It looks lovely. As it usually does when she's finished up.

The house got a total overhaul, she called it, twice a year. Framed artwork was taken down, and the walls were given a good scrubbing. The paper or paint would be replaced then too if it needed it. The house smelled like Murphy's Oil Soap and Windex.

Benson was taken to the library and asked if he wanted anything to drink. He did, a large bottle of whiskey, but he'd given up on trying to drink away his depression a couple of days ago. He'd been sleeping better since then. Telling Billy he'd like a glass of tea, the man went to get it for him. Benson, too nervous to sit, walked around the room looking at things he knew had been in the room for decades, but he'd not noticed before.

"You've no idea how many times I've wanted to trash that ugly thing since your mother gave it to us for our first anniversary. How are you, Benny?" He kissed his wife on the cheek and sat when she did. "I wanted to talk to you about a few things. Mostly, I wanted to see if you'd like to come back home. I think—no, I know that I might have flown off the handle just a little too quickly."

"You didn't. You were right about me being a screw up." She looked as surprised as he'd been when he came to realize the same thing. "I want to come back. I miss you. But I don't want to run the company. Not alone. I think you'd be better at the job than I ever was."

"That is certainly nothing I thought you'd say." He nodded and pulled out his notes. "You've written things down? My goodness, Benny, what has happened to you?"

"Something that should have happened to me decades ago. I've also had a long conversation with the programmer that I screwed around with. She's been more than generous with taking our company back." Denise told him she'd spoken to her as well. "Good. Her name eludes me right now, but her programs were top notch. We, or you, should have them in all the businesses that your family owned." Denise told him her name. "That's right. Piper. I've spoken to her several times, as a matter of fact. I've gone over some of the things I began to notice that should be changed. Only after making a complete fool of myself trying to hardball her. She's a stubborn little thing."

Denise laughed. "She is at that. When I told her that you and I were going to talk, she told me I'd better have a damned good reason for not allowing you back in the company. Apparently, she's been hearing about the things you've been doing. Piper told me you were talking to other companies about getting their security checked." He said he was careful not to name any one company when doing that. "I heard that. I don't know why you'd not mention her company since you think it lived up to what you wanted it to do. But she told me you'd been very busy."

"If she heard what I was doing, I didn't want her to think I was only doing it because I wanted to get back in her good graces." He laughed then. "Not that I think it would have worked. She isn't one to pull any punches when she thinks you're a screw up. I don't think she was always that way."

"No. I remember talking to her when the program was being designed. She was so timid sounding. Like she was afraid of her own shadow. Now she's a ballbuster, making sure the people she works with are on top of things." Benson nodded. "I do want you to come home. I've discovered I miss fussing at you. And as I said before, I think I was too harsh when the entire thing with the business started to fall apart."

"You were right, Denise. I was a bastard. I know I was to a great many people." He opened his list up. "These are some of the people I'm going to make amends to. As soon as I'm able. They're mostly people in the trade that we dealt with that I was rude to. I can't believe I ever thought that was a good way to run a business."

"I've been paying off some of the debts we owe, but I'm having trouble with that. I don't think people are going to be as open armed with us as they might have been before. We're both going to have to work on that, I think." She smiled at him. "I might have lost my temper a time or two myself. People will take a mile if you give them an inch. I'm not very good at hearing how badly you might have treated people. I wanted to tell them to just shut the hell up and take the damned money. Finally, I had to have someone else do it for me. It was just too much to think about all the time."

"If I'd been doing my job correctly all along, you wouldn't have been put in that position at all. I'm not saying I was wrong about everything I did, but pretty close if you want to know the truth. I had a wonderful profitable company, and I nearly ruined it all by being an asshole. I'm still working on becoming a better man. Not just for the company, but for you as well." Denise took his hand into hers. "Denise, I'd like to start anew with you too. We need to do things together again. Go out and enjoy a nice meal someplace. I've been keeping up with Piper on a couple of things too. Did you know she's putting together care boxes for the men and women in prison? I think we could do something like that, but with the children going to school. Supplies that they might not be able to get. Things for the teachers' rooms as well. Then there is the homeless shelter. I spent a few hours there just yesterday morning, handing out food and making sure there are enough things to go around."

"I can't imagine you being in a soup kitchen, Benny. Whatever will the neighbors say?" He told her what he should say to them. "Yes, well, that might be a good idea, in theory, to make them come help, but I doubt Mr. Graves is going to be doing anyone any good if he gets there and has a stroke. The man is ninety-five years old. Oh, to be in that good of shape when I reach his age."

"What are you talking about? You're beautiful right now. You're only going to be more beautiful as you grow old with me." Denise thanked him. "I do want to be more of a help to the community rather than someone that takes advantage of things. I've been sitting on my lazy bum all my life. I want to make a difference in some lives, damn it."

They talked for the next couple of hours. Benson had forgotten what a great sense of humor Denise had. It was also very sharp. They talked about trips they'd never taken. The things they wanted to do for the town. He even convinced her to have a company Christmas party this year with all the employees. It would mean shutting down their company for a whole day, but he thought in the long run, it would be well worth it.

Billy asked if he was staying for dinner, and Benson turned to Denise. He would not assume anything with her anymore. Had he listened to her from the first, he would have been a better man than he was now. Benson had learned a great deal with his walks through the town, as well as a few places he might not have ever thought of going before all this happened.

"He'll be moving back in with us, Billy. What do you think of that?" Billy smiled and asked if he was ready to get rid of all his suits. "Suits? Yes, I think that's a splendid idea. Not all of them, but most. We both need to be more approachable, too, I think. Let people see us as people they can come too."

Getting rid of his suits was only the first step in making them more approachable. Benson had worn a suit to the soup shelter and had not one person come up and ask him for a thing. But when he'd worn his jeans and a T-shirt, people would talk to him about most anything. Granted, some of it wasn't anything he wanted to know about a person, but it was nice knowing the clothing he wore made a difference right away in how he was treated. Also, how he treated others.

"I've discovered things about myself, Denise. Not all of it was bad, as I'm sure you're thinking." She laughed and shook her head. "I'm not as impatient as I was only a week ago. I'm taking time to smell the roses, so to speak. I've been listening to people rather than trying to find a way to rid myself of them. Did you know there are many ways to fix a pair of shoes so that you can get at least another year out of them? Yes, I can tell you that I could afford new ones, but I was told I needed to make a smaller footprint in the world. I'm ashamed to say I had to go and look that up after I was lectured about it. And he was right. I think we all need to make a smaller print of ourselves in this old world. It is the only one we have."

Benson also thought about the little creature that had come to see him in his hotel room. A little person by the name of Toby. It did, admittedly, take him an entire day to figure out he wasn't having a stroke or something. However, once the little man started telling him things he could do for all the world, Benson realized he was right.

On his list was making a park in the middle of the town square, a place for flowers to grow. Some benches so that people could sit and admire them. Benson was going to do his best to bring more jobs to town. To make sure that once the people started working again, there were places for them to go and do local shopping. His head was swimming with all the things he wanted to do. Not for himself this time, but for the entire world.

Toby pointed out to him over and over, you only have one life to live. And how you lived it and died by it would determine how you were remembered.

"Do you want people to say, 'There goes Mr. Alexander, the cheapest bastard that ever lived'? Or do you want them to go, 'Sure gonna miss that old geezer. He sure could throw a great party.'" Benson then admitted that he didn't have the slightest clue how to even throw a party. That was when Toby told him he'd be right there with him. All the time. Then when the time was right, Toby would introduce his wife to her faerie.

Toby had all sorts of odd sayings too. But his favorite one was *Man is not measured by the size of his suit, but his willingness to get it dirty for someone else.* Benson was going to get this put on a hat or something. It was going to be his mantra for the rest of his life.

# Chapter 10

Collier was ready to jump into the seat as soon as Emmie was finished backing it into the slot. He knew this was deceptive, but there wasn't any other way for him to make any money than to tweak the system once in a while. Not cheat. He'd never cheat someone, but he would tweak things so he could feed his family. What little there was of it.

"Okay, Dad. You're there." Emmie moved to the back of the truck and sat quietly on the bed. She and her little girl, Olivia, were depending on him to make this work. It had been a long time since he'd been a trucker. Even longer since he'd tweaked the system. "Just be calm."

Calm? Collier hadn't been calm in decades. Emmie and Olivia had moved in with him. They'd had to, as his little world had taken such a brutal hit that he'd nearly not made it out on the sunshine side. He looked down at the picture near the speedometer and had to smile.

There wasn't anything like having a granddaughter. Olivia would only need to put her hand on his shoulder, and he'd know things would be all right. At fourteen, she was now the exact age as her mother when she had gotten pregnant with her. That, too, had nearly killed him.

His little girl being kidnapped and raped had been what started him on the downward spiral of feeling like a failure. Not only that, but he'd been unable to cope with important things anymore. Nor the little things. As he sat there at the wheel of the semi, he gave himself a moment to reflect while the back end of his truck was being loaded.

Collier was a drunk. His morning meal had been a glass—not a shot, but a full water glass—of whatever booze had been at hand. Then he'd go out into the barn, a place filled with so many familiar smells that he'd sit out there drinking again until he was called into dinner. After he'd had his fill of whatever was on the table, he'd drink until he was too drunk to climb the stairs. Until one horrific night when his wife had fallen down the stairs and died.

He'd been no more than five inches from her body when he'd stumbled out of his chair that next morning and found her. Not understanding or even sober enough to know what to do, he spent most of the morning trying to wake her. It wasn't until Emmie came down from her room, a little tyke back then, that the police were called by her. By then, of course, the die was set.

Emmie wouldn't speak to him for weeks after. She had

placed the blame of her mother being gone squarely where it belonged—right on his head. It occurred to him several days later that in his effort to get his only child to speak to him, at ten, she was already a stubborn force to contend with. He'd not had a single drink. When he went to look for just a sip, as he told himself, every bottle he located had been emptied. Emmie had done that.

"You take another drink, and I'll leave you." He pointed out that she was a child. "I'm more of an adult than you are, Dad. Momma taught me how to take care of things. I'm smart, but I'm also gonna be mean. You drink even one more drink, and I'll run away, and you'll die here all alone. Is that what you want?"

"No. But I need it." She had a suitcase packed already, and picked it up and went to the door. "You're not being fair, Emmie. I just lost my wife."

"And I lost my mom. The only person in this house that cared enough to get up in the morning and make sure I had food in my belly. You're not going to be able to do that with you drinking all the time." He didn't like the way she was speaking to him, but knew to point that out would have her out the door before he could get to her. Collier asked her to be fair. "Fair would have been for you to have fallen down the stairs and broken your neck, Dad. Mom, at least, could cook. You're a drunk. I can't be keeping you from falling too if I'm to go to school so I can be someone you and Mom can be proud of."

"You want that? For me to be proud of you?" Emmie

had nodded, her little curls bobbing to the way her head bounced. "You'll have to help me, Emmie. I've been too long in the bottle to just stop now."

"You've been sober for five weeks, Dad. I'm sure you're past the point of needing it again." She put her suitcase down, the one that said she was going places and looked at him with her arms crossed over her tiny chest. "Do we have a deal? I'm not going to have time to make sure you're going to be alive when I come home from school. Also, if you want me to grow up, you're going to have to learn some things. Get back on the road too."

"How will I watch over you if I'm on the road?" She gave him a look that she'd perfected over the years since then. "All right. You can take care of yourself. But it's only until we can get back on our feet. All right?"

"Of course. Whatever you want." That statement had been the biggest lie she'd ever told him. He realized now that she could maneuver him as well as she did this big rig into places he might not have thought he could go.

Collier nearly screamed a little when someone knocked on his window.

"Mr. Rankin?" Collier nodded as he rolled down his window. "Good. You have three stops on this load. All the information is right there on the inventory sheet. Like we said when we hired you, if you do this first job without any trouble, we'll keep you on to keep delivering for us. All right?"

"Yes, Mr. Prince. Thank you." He remembered just

then the question that Emmie had asked him to find out. "Why is it you don't want to hire women? I mean, it's fine; however you want to do this, but why no women?"

"You'll see that you're delivering to prisons. This isn't a mandate from us, but the board of directors of each of the jails. They don't want women in the trucks in the event that some of the men, the ones that will be unloading the trucks, get an idea in their heads that they can overpower one of them and get out. It's been my experience with my wife and sisters-in-law that they can fight harder than a man if cornered. But I'm not the one in charge."

It was a good answer. One that he was sure Emmie would still tear apart. But he did like the fact that the man didn't necessarily agree with the findings. Putting his paperwork on the seat next to him, Collier pulled away from the dock and onto the road leading out of the new building.

When Emmie sat down on the seat, she picked up the paperwork. Olivia, he could see, was in the back working on something on the floor. Collier could drive long enough to get them out of town, but his nerves wouldn't allow him to get them onto the highway toward their first stop. Emmie was looking over the paperwork when he asked her if she thought it was a good run.

"It is. The pay is better than I would have gotten if it had only been a drop and go at even a larger chain. I know this is donated items for the prisoners, but they're spending a great deal of money on getting it there." Olivia told them both how much. The smile that both him and her mother gave her made his heart sing. "Yes, quite a bit. Thanks for asking him about the women, Dad. I guess that does make sense if you think about it."

"It does." When she turned away from him, he saw the scar, one that he was sure his daughter saw every time she looked in the mirror. A scar that had nearly ended all their lives. There was no way he could have lived without his little girl. And then his granddaughter. "I like the fact that it's a one day and done delivery. That way, we can be home every night and not have to be out on the open road."

"Nothing would have happened to us had we had to. We'd have been safe locked up in here overnight." He knew that in his head, but his heart and nerves thought differently. "Did you take your medication today?"

"I did. Before we left the house." She nodded and read over the paperwork they'd been given. "Daughter, do you suppose when this is up and going, you could try and work with me again to get me driving on the highway?"

Her smile, always something he looked for, turned to him. "Yes. You know I'll do whatever you want." He laughed a little, still his little maneuver. "What's so funny?"

"Nothing. I was just thinking how Olivia says that now too. She no more means it than you do. Whatever I want simply means whatever you think is best for me. You've been the parent in this relationship since you came to me with that little suitcase filled with all your things." Collier laughed again. "You know, I really thought you'd only been threatening me that day and had yourself an empty case. I nearly sobbed when I saw how you'd packed all your little things so neatly in it. When I asked you about your dolls, you told me if you were having to live on your own, you didn't have time for frivolous things. Such a big word for such a little girl, I thought."

"I'm glad you didn't test me on it. I haven't any idea where I might have gone that day. To the barn, I suppose." She turned away from him again, he knew, so he'd not see the sadness there. "Dad, did you hate me for treating you that way? I've never been as scared as I was back then that you'd take drink over me."

"I've never hated anything about you, love. Never in all my life, since I held you in my arms, has anyone meant as much to me as you do. Then you know what you went and did? You gave me a second chance at being a good person when you laid that little one back there in my arms." Olivia pointed out that she could hear them, and she wasn't little. "No, neither of you are anymore, are you?"

"No. But that doesn't mean we don't still need you in our lives." He drove to their home, a place where they'd pack up what little they'd need, and then Emmie would take over. Before he'd left the Prince Foundation today, he'd gotten permission to stop by his home for a few things.

They really didn't need all that much. Just bottles of water, something for Olivia to snack on, as well as some changes of clothing. He was of the opinion that everywhere they went, there had to be something to change into. It had come from his nerves.

He wasn't just nervous all the time. It was just what they called it now. Collier suffered from depression. Not just being sad, but major chronic depression, or MCD, which would plague him for days on end if he didn't take his medication. It was, he knew, getting harder and harder to keep himself in control. But having the little things he needed around him and someone accepting of them was what he needed when things were really bad.

The clothing was one of them. If he was feeling particularly down, he'd only go and slip on something else. It didn't have to be much different than what he had on. Even if it was only the color of his pants, he would put them on as his happy clothing. So in changing, his head would associate his putting them on as a change. A change that he could deal with.

Then there were the games. Collier wasn't a person that would sit and play games a lot. Rarely before his wife had died had he had time. Drinking had taken up any time he'd had free, or when he should have been working. But now he had three games he would play. A car game, a trucking game, and a game he played at home. They were simple, yet very effective.

As Emmie drove, he would say his alphabet frontwards then backwards until the need to throw himself from a moving truck passed. That, too, was getting harder and harder to keep in control. He looked at Emmie when she changed lanes.

"I was wondering if you'd given any thought to the idea of moving." Emmie looked at him, then back at the road, asking him if he had. "I have. Not as much as I should have, I think, but I have thought about it. Moving into another home, the doctor told me, might be just what I need, or it might trigger something that will harm me. I'm afraid to find out. Are you?"

"Yes. And no. I think his idea about going to see homes was a good idea. So long as you're in charge of the actual being able to buy the house. I'm not to influence you in any way about it." Collier wasn't sure he thought that was a good idea. He was getting up there, and it would be Emmie that would have it after he was gone. "There isn't any rush on it, Dad. You know as well as I that we could stay where we are for the rest of our lives and be happy. But as you've pointed out, the house isn't really big enough for the three of us with only two bedrooms. I have the money to buy us whatever we want. And as Olivia pointed out, we can always add to the one we have. It's up to you." She looked at him. "Whatever you want to do."

They all three laughed. Olivia came up from the back and kissed him on the cheek. She'd not move around the truck too much when they were on the road, but he was always ready for a quick hug or kiss from them. Somehow it was like getting a supercharge from an electrical outlet when they did that for him.

They were at the jail by ten in the morning. Like Emmie

had backed him in to be loaded up, she did the same when they delivered. This time, he had to get out of the truck to make sure the seals were put on, and that the prisoners unloading the truck only took what belonged to them. Collier watched them carefully, his nerves getting the better of him as he stood there watching the men unload the truck.

~*~

"Damn it, breathe, Dad." She didn't want to hit him, but it was that, or they were going to call an ambulance for him. "Dad, if you don't wake up, I'm going to hit you hard enough to wake you from the dead. Wake up."

The slap, more than likely harder than she should have hit him, brought him around. Falling back on her ass when he sat up gasping for breath, all she could think about was what would have happened had she not been keeping an eye on him while he'd been out of the truck.

"You all right, Mr. Rankin?" He nodded. Dad was staring at her like he was upset. She knew just what he was thinking—that he'd embarrassed her. He'd not. She stood up when one of the people off the dock came down to help her dad up. "You gave us a scare there, sir. You going to be all right now?"

"Yes. The heat." It was less than fifty degrees out, so everyone knew he hadn't passed out because of any heat. "I just get myself nervous and forget to take in as much air as I'm putting out. That's all."

"We'd never hurt you. I hope you know that." The

man, a big guy with numbers printed across his T-shirt, looked at her. "You all right, miss? You looked as terrified as anything I'd ever seen."

"He's my dad." Emmie had told her daughter not to move when she'd leapt out to get Dad. Glancing back at the truck, she thought of the excuse they'd made up if they were caught with her there. "My car broke down a few miles back, and Dad was good enough to pick me up. I'm not usually with him when he's out."

The man nodded, but she had a feeling he wasn't buying it. Instead of trying to make her case, which she was sure would make it worse, she got up and went back to the truck. Once he was checked out by their doctor, him telling her dad to take it easy, they were well on their way to the next stop when his phone rang.

"Mr. Rankin, I hope you're feeling better." Dad had put it on speakerphone before it rang. He looked at her when the woman told him that her name was Piper Prince. "I'm not mad, so please don't take it that way, but I would have liked to have known that you had your daughter with you. It might well have saved me some embarrassment when I got a call from the prison a few minutes ago."

Dad had her pull over, and he sat there, sobbing out their lies while she held him. He also told her how they needed this job because of the fact that he was an ill man. Emmie immediately hated the woman for what she'd done to her dad.

"Mrs. Prince, this is entirely my fault. I wanted to

spend some time with my dad, and I sort of talked him into us coming." Piper told her to call her by her first name and not to lie to her. "Mrs. Prince, I'm beginning to see a part of you that I'm not particularly fond of. And I won't call you by your given name any more than I would call my dad by his first name. I'll have him take us home, and we'll be—"

"Us?" She looked at her daughter and waited for a moment before she said anything about her. "You have your child there with you. Oh, that must be so much fun for your dad and you. To have three generations in one truck. I'll tell you what I'm going to do. I'm going to call the next place you are to hit and tell them that Mr. Rankin has taken ill and that you'll be driving. That way, they can prepare themselves for you being there. Then when you come back here for the next load, we'll have dinner together. Your family and mine."

"No." The woman laughed at her answer, or she was off her noddle. Either way, Emmie wasn't going to get all warm and fuzzy with them. She told her it was fuzzy, not fuzzed. "Are you reading my mind? That's beyond rude, you know that, don't you?"

"I do. I wouldn't have to if you were to tell me what I want to know. Also, I feel pretty good about the fact you didn't know I was doing it. I'm getting better at it as I go on. But as for dinner, I'm making arrangements now with the family. I have a feeling you're going to be stubborn no matter how much I beg, so let me just say that you'll have dinner with us, all of you, or your father is out of a job. I've been looking into things while I have been talking to you, and I know all about your family, Emmie. I'm sorry, but I must insist that the three of you come here so we can talk. That's nothing that is going to hurt any of you." Dad nodded but looked defeated. The hatred for this woman was piling up more and more. "Don't do that. Don't judge me for something I'm trying to help you with, Emmie. Deliver the other two loads and come back here for dinner."

There wasn't any way she could turn her down when this job was needed. They didn't need the money. They were doing just fine. But in order to get a home loan if they went that way or even a construction loan, she needed to have some sort of job to prove she could make the payments. Being self-employed, even with making the money she was, there wasn't any way the bank would lend them money.

"We'll be there. It's not going to be a friendly or a happy occasion for either of us. Just to give you a heads up, I don't like to be blackmailed any more than I'm sure you would." Piper asked her if they had anything they were allergic to. "My daughter doesn't eat meat. Of any kind."

"I can work with that. By the way, there is something you need to know. The males of this family are all tigers. They do eat meat. So is your daughter going to be upset if those around her eat meat?" Olivia answered her for herself. "Right. Just you don't eat it. Good to know. I'm happy to be meeting the three of you. I know we're going to be the best of friends. In saying that, I've sent along a little person to help you three. His name is Pudge. Just don't squash him when you see him."

"I'm sorry. What?" Piper explained how he was a faerie. "Why are you sending us a faerie? This is getting more and more complicated all the time. Why don't we just call it quits, and I'll find someplace else to work."

"There aren't any openings for you, Emmie. We both know that. You're much too smart for the people you work with, and you don't have the patience to deal with stupidity. I believe you're smart enough to realize we can help each other in what we both have going on. My family could use a good attorney, and you might just fit the bill in that department."

"I'm not a practicing attorney anymore." Piper pointed out she'd just renewed her license, so that told her she was an attorney. "You're very informed for someone we don't know. I want you to stay the hell out of my head."

"As I said before. I would if you were more forthcoming than you've been." Emmie started the truck and moved out into the traffic again. She was going to get this shit done, then go to the house and tell them all to fuck off. "I think we're going to get along just fine, Emmie. Just fine indeed."

The next place they stopped knew that she was the one driving. Not only did they make a better time than she had anticipated, but Pudge showed up. He was in the truck, entertaining Olivia when she got back on the road. Her dad had been silent since the phone call ended an hour ago.

Emmie didn't mind the long silences that came with driving a truck. She'd worked her way through college doing this, and was debt free by the time she'd gotten her doctorate in law. Olivia had been her road partner since the day she'd been born, and Emmie got her license to drive the big rigs.

While her dad dealt with his thoughts, she thought about what had happened since the day she'd been able to escape the monster that held her for those terrible, nightmarish three days when she'd turned fourteen.

Like any other teenager, Emmie loved to ride her bike. Her dad and she had had a slight disagreement about her birthday that was coming up, so she'd taken off to blow off some steam. She'd wanted to skip it, and he wanted to go all out. Emmie didn't have the heart to tell him people didn't like her much, and inviting anyone to her party would be hard as she had not one single friend.

The man had been trying his best to get a kid into his van when she rode up on them. Hurting the man, kicking him in the nuts, she told the little boy to run. And damn, but he had run. Before she could do the same, she was hit from behind and lost out on the little window of opportunity to get away.

For three days, he beat the shit out of her. He'd not raped her or even touched her sexually. He was only hurting her because she'd taken away his prize, what he'd called the kid that had gotten away.

He'd not only not let her go to use the bathroom, which ended up with her standing in her own pee, but he didn't feed her either. She was nearly too weak when the opportunity presented itself to get away, to make her way out of the basement to the police. The man never once touched her. It was his son that had fathered Olivia.

He'd found her in the basement when his dad had gone out. She had always wondered if it was to pick up another boy. The son came to the basement that day, cut her loose, and raped her repeatedly until his dad returned. The apple hadn't fallen that far from the tree, apparently.

When the kid's dad returned and saw what he'd done, they argued brutally. Getting up from the floor, grabbing anything she touched to pull over her naked body, Emmie was nearly up the stairs when the first of many gunshots were fired.

"Mom?" Pulling from her thoughts was difficult—it always had been when she found herself reliving the day. Smiling at her daughter while keeping an eye on the road, she asked her what she needed. "Do you think we can pull over in that gas station? I have to go to the bathroom."

"Sure. Just let me get over." As she was making the turn into the large pull off, she spoke to Olivia. "You know the rules, don't you? I mean, I know you know them, but you'll follow them, right?"

Nodding, she had to laugh when Olivia jumped out of

the truck and was racing to the building even as she turned off the engine. Dad must have been sleeping because he woke up slightly confused. She told him what they were doing.

"I should go too." Dad got out of the truck and stretched. Emmie did the same, stretching while still in the truck. "Would you like to have a couple of drinks while I'm in here? I could sure use something besides water."

She told Dad some juice would be great and that she was going to top off the tank. One thing that they'd gotten from the company they were working for was a gas card. Not that she used it, but she did keep the receipt in the event they asked. Olivia joined her just as she was pulling the handle off the tank.

"While Grandda is gone, can I ask you something?" Emmie said she could always ask her anything. "Grandda is really ill, isn't he? I mean, he seems to be upset more and more all the time. Don't you think?"

"Yes. I think the next time he goes to the doctor, they're going to up his meds even more. I worry about him a great deal." Olivia nodded but only stood there. "What else, Olivia? Something else is bothering you. What is it?"

"These people you're working for? The ones that called you today? I don't know that I like the way she spoke to you. It sort of makes me mad enough to beg you not to go there. I don't know why, but I have a feeling something terrible is going to come about." Emmie thought about what her daughter had said. "Are you mad at me for saying that?"

"Goodness no. I was thinking about a way to talk to you without dropping the F-bomb about three hundred times." Emmie was glad for the smile. "I don't like it either, and I wouldn't have to be begged if we didn't need this job. You understand that, don't you? We need to get Grandpa out of that house. The doctor said there are too many memories bringing him down."

"I think it's more than that." While waiting in line to pay for her gasoline, Dad joined her with several bottles of juice. Then Olivia went and got some bags of things to eat too. If nothing else happened today, she was sure they were going to be upset when they had dinner at the Prince home. "I would also like five dollars, please."

Instead of asking her what she wanted it for, Emmie handed it over. Olivia didn't ask for much, so when she did, Emmie knew that it was something that she really wanted. She and Dad both kept an eye on her as she made her way to the man that was outside with his kids in a well-used van.

Emmie was ready to leap at her daughter to get her away from the van when her dad left her to see to her. When she'd paid for her gas, she went out to the van with the two of them. Pudge landed on her shoulder and started to speak to her quietly.

"They've no money, miss. It's going to be hard for him to feed his little family and move closer to where he's headed." Emmie asked him where they were going. "He's going to go to Florida, if he can get there, to find himself a good job. His wife left him several months ago, leaving behind not just large bills for him to pay off, but three small children as well."

"Is this real or a test, Pudge? I don't want any of what I do to get back to the Prince family. If you're here to keep an eye on me, I'd just as soon you'd leave now." He assured her it was real, and that he'd only told her because he thought her curious. "You'll not tell them if I help or not?"

"'Tis your business, miss. If you don't want them to know, I shan't say a word." Nodding, she moved toward the man. "Miss. Do you think it would be all right if I were to go to the flowers over there? I've not eaten today."

"You do what you need to do, Pudge. And you should have told me you were hungry. I would have fed you what you wanted." He told her he was sorry and stood on her shoulder as she spoke to the man. "If you'd pull your van over to the pumps, sir, I'd be happy to fill your tank for you."

"You'd do that?" She nodded and helped him get the children in their car seats. "It's been a long journey for us, I'm afraid."

"Pudge, can you fix his car for him?" He told her it would be his pleasure. He could also make it so he'd not need gas again until he reached his destination. "Yes, well, I have an idea for that as well. Just get his car in better shape for him."

When the man left her to head to her home, Emmie

was happy that she'd been able to help. Feeding his family had been a blast when the kids argued over who got to sit on Olivia's lap while they ate.

"Raymond, you go to the house and get the key where I told you it was. Then you and your children settle in, and I'll be back in a couple of days. The house has been sitting too long without anyone in it." It was her grandma's home. She'd left it to her when she'd passed away. "You can start working for me then. All right?"

He hugged her, crying about how nice she was being to him. Instead of letting him hug her again, she pushed him on his way. They were all back in the truck a few minutes later, onto the last leg of their journey today. Then on to the Prince family.

# Chapter 11

Kylan was running behind, as usual. He had been at his apartment cleaning out his fridge when he was told they were having dinner together tonight. Just as he was finishing his clean up, Summer came to speak to him.

"Your house is complete, sir." He looked at Summer and asked her what she was talking about. "Your mate. I've been to see her, and she has wonderful ideas about your home you'll share with her. I'd not be surprised if she were to fall in love with you this night."

"I don't have a mate, Summer." She smiled at him. "How do you know what my mate wants in a house when I don't know a thing about her? In addition to that, what do you mean, she'll fall in love with me this night? I don't have any plans to leave the house."

"She is coming with her family for dinner tonight. Lady Piper spoke with her just today." Kylan asked her what that had to do with him. "Why everything, my lord.

You'll be so happy with her daughter as well. Your mate's daddy, he is most ill, but we can fix him up when he is ready."

Kylan sat down and thought about what she was telling him. "What's her name?" Summer asked him if he meant her daughter or his mate. "Both. For that matter, who told you she was my mate?"

"I know these things. But it was Lady Piper that told me about her. She is so very beautiful, sir. Her hair is like the sunshine, it is so bright. Her daughter has dark hair like yours. Also, your mate—her name is Emmaline, but her dad calls her Emmie—has one blue eye and one green eye. She covers it with contacts, but even without them showing, she is very lovely. A perfect match for you."

Now he was headed to Fisher's home for dinner and to meet his mate. The big rig in the drive of their home was the first indication of what she did for a living. Going to the back door, not wanting to be pushed into something that was wrong, he saw Piper there waiting on him. She looked too slick for his tastes.

"Summer told you, didn't she?" He asked Piper if it was true. "It is. She's very outspoken, but nice when it suits her." She told him about the man who was now working for her.

"How are you finding this out, Piper? Did you get some sort of vision magic that you've not told anyone about?" She grinned and told him she had. "Is she going to be happy to find out I'm her mate? Or are we going to have a battle on our hands? Is her family going to come around and beat me up too?"

"The only family she has is her father and daughter. The father of her daughter, Olivia, is dead, killed by his father when he raped Emmie when she was only fourteen years old." Kylan sat down at the table in the kitchen, waiting for the next part of Piper's tale. He knew there was more to it than she was saying, but he didn't ask. "There is no one chasing them—no bad people after them. They're not wealthy like you are, but they have learned to stretch a dollar until it screams, as her dad says. There isn't a bad skeleton in their closet that they're going to keep from anyone. Collier, her father, is a recovering drunk, but has been sober for nearly eighteen years. They're just a family that has had some bad things happen to them, but they've recovered nicely."

"Who else knows she's my mate other than the three of us?" She told him she'd not even told Fisher yet. "What's going on here, Piper? I don't know why, but I have a feeling things aren't as cut and dried as you've made them out to be."

"She's an attorney. A damned good one too." Nodding, he told her he and his brothers had been attorneys several times over their lives. "Emmie specializes in corporate law. Like I said, she's damned good at it too. We need her in this family as much as you're going to need her as your mate."

"I don't understand this." She told him that was all

right. He would. "You've told me I have a mate, then leave me hanging about why she's so important to this family. That's not very sisterly of you."

"No, I suppose it's not. What if I told you she needs to be a part of this family so you can save her father's life? Make him have a good feeling about himself." Kylan told her he could do that without taking a mate. "Why are you being so obtuse about this? I'm trying to do the right thing here and not give you too much information before you've met."

"Is that important?" Piper nodded. "All right. I'll not ask you anymore about her. But I do have to know, why is it that you've told me this? I can understand you've got rules about not telling too much of what the future holds, but you've told me a great deal."

When her house phone rang, she told him it was for him. Going to the phone, he picked it up and said his name. He heard the words being said to him, but he was having a difficult time making them into information after the first comment. After telling the officer where he was and how long he'd been there, he hung up the phone.

"My apartment complex blew up forty minutes ago." She didn't say anything but did hand him a glass of water. "Everything is gone. No one was home, so they're all safe. You knew this. Didn't you?"

"When I saw what happened, I knew I had to get you from the house. You would have been there had I only invited you to dinner. You would have come here, but it would have been too late for you to get out. So I told you of your mate so you'd leave early enough not to be there when the boiler burst." He nodded. "It was the only way, Kylan. I didn't know what else to do. I can't see you hurt."

"Thank you." He thought about what she'd said to him. "You said I have to save her father's life. Was that it? Did he come to my apartment too?"

"No. He needs you in another way."

Getting up, he staggered a little but made his way to the living room. He saw Olivia first. If she looked only half like her mom, he was going to be in deep trouble with the beautiful women to come into his life.

Kylan hugged his mom and dad, introduced himself to Collier, and sat down on the couch where his brothers were. He looked at Emmie as she spoke to Harper about the runs that she'd taken out for them today. When Emmie looked at him, Kylan knew he'd been wrong. He was going to be in more than just trouble with his new mate, he was going to be running around with his tongue hanging out whenever he saw her. Christ, she was more than beautiful. She was gorgeous.

The poke to his ribs had him looking at his mom. "You're staring at her like you're going to eat her alive. If you keep that up, young man, she's going to hurt you." He looked at his mom. "I've only just met her, but I have a feeling she won't hold back if you do something to cause her trouble. Is she your mate?"

"Yes." Mom nodded and leaned back on the couch,

pulling him back with her. "She's beautiful, isn't she? I mean, all women are beautiful, but she's...she's beyond that."

"What the hell is wrong with you?" He looked back at the woman they'd been speaking of. "You're staring at me like I'm some sort of shit under your foot. Either say what you have to say or stop looking at me like that."

"You're my mate." There was a deafening silence in the room. "I only just found out myself. You're very beautiful."

When Emmie stood up, he did as well. Not only was she good looking, but she was also nearly as tall as he was. He'd estimate she was at least six feet, if not a little more. Before he could pull her to him, if he had that thought in his head, Olivia stood between them. She was shooting daggers at him with her eyes.

"Hello." Olivia didn't so much as utter a single word to him. "I'm Kylan Prince. You must be her daughter."

"I'm the spitting image of my mother. If you don't back off right now, mister, I don't know people's space bubble—I'm gonna hurt you. I've been trained by the best there is in defending myself and others." He smiled at her and told Olivia he was glad to know that. "You won't be if you're picking up your nuts from across the room."

"Now, see here." Mom got up and came to stand by him and his new family members. "You might be able to speak that way at home, young lady, but you will hold your tongue on—"

"She's not allowed to speak like that anywhere." Emmie told Olivia to apologize to Mrs. Prince. When she did, Olivia also told her that her mother raised her better than that. "I'm going to keep right on raising her better than you did this moron. Not that I'm blaming you. I guess not everyone takes to being a good person like the rest of your family apparently has."

"Kylan does have his days. How about we all have a seat, then we can see what there is to know about the rest of you." Alarm ran over his body when he heard one of his brothers calling to Collier. Moving toward the man, he could see that not only were his eyes glazed over in apparent pain, but his lips were blue. Kylan heard his mother speak as he was helping Collier to the floor. "Call an ambulance. Be quick about it."

Taking off the tie he had on, Kylan spoke to the elder man. He told him what he was doing with each step that he took. Emmie was on the other side of her dad, telling him to open his mouth. Before he could do what she wanted, his eyes closed, and Kylan knew the man was going to need more than just his help, but everyone's.

Performing CPR, he didn't stop until Emmie said it was her turn. Before the ambulance arrived, two of his brothers had helped with the rotation. Not that he couldn't have done it for a lot longer, but he didn't want to mess up by hurting her father while he was trying to save him.

The EMTs came in with their equipment and switched off with him when they had his chest exposed. It only took them seconds to hit him with the defibrillator and bring the man back. They were hooking Collier up to an IV and calling in his vitals when Olivia came and hugged him.

"He's my grandda. And besides my mom, all I have in the world. You saved him for me." Holding her as he stood up, he wasn't the least bit surprised to see Emmie sitting on the couch now with her head between her knees. "Can you talk to my mom? Don't touch her. She'll scream if you do. Just talk to her and not touch her."

Kylan didn't understand the no touching part, but he did sit on the couch with Emmie and spoke to her. He wasn't telling her anything substantial, but just telling her what the EMTs were doing as they worked to keep her father alive. When Emmie sat up, he asked her if she was all right.

"I should have noticed he wasn't well." Kylan said those closest to people sometimes didn't see things. He was guilty of the same thing. "Don't pamper me with niceties. I should have noticed he wasn't feeling well when we drove here today. He said his head hurt and that his belly was upset. If you think you might have even the slightest chance of making me your mate, you'll never lie to me or try and sugarcoat things that are going on. I won't have it."

"All right. I had a little bit of a warning when I got here that he might need me. I was on top of it because of that." She asked him if it had been Piper. "It was. She and my brother work for some very powerful people, the queen of the earth, Aurora, and she gifted them with all kinds of magic. That's me not sugarcoating things. Why did your daughter tell me not to touch you?"

"I've been raped before, and sometimes I have trouble with sudden moves and touches. What did she tell you about us?" He told her about the explosion and the reason he was told about her. "So you only know I'm your mate because someone told you I was. Is that the way it works?"

"No. I can smell you. Your scent calls to me. It also warns other males, other cats, that you're a mate to someone powerful." She asked him what that meant. "I'm a very old and very powerful tiger. Black tiger, as a matter of fact."

"I won't give up my daughter without a fight. And I'm including death to you if you even try." He said he'd never ever do that to her or to Olivia. "We'll see. I have to go to the hospital. My dad is going to need me. He's on all kinds of antidepressants."

"May I go? The hospital might need me to answer some questions about what happened." She told him to suit himself. "Will Olivia want to go?"

"I'm not leaving her alone with strangers." But in the end, Olivia wanted to stay. Kylan knew it was costing Emmie to leave her only child there, but Olivia said she'd be fine and was stressed out too much to wait on someone to tell them what was going on. "All right. But you know the rules and what to do."

"I do, Mom. I'll be fine."

His mom didn't say anything, but he could tell she was

curious. He was as well, but he didn't ask either of them what the rules were. Instead, he got his car so that Emmie could ride with him to the hospital. He had a feeling it was going to be a long night. Kylan only hoped it was going to be a good night rather than snipping at him like she had been doing.

Although, he was enjoying her show of temper.

**Before You Go...**

# HELP AN AUTHOR

## *write a review*

# THANK YOU!

Share your voice and help guide other readers to these wonderful books. Even if it's only a line or two, your reviews help readers discover the author's books so they can continue creating stories that you'll love. Log in to your favorite retailer and leave a review. Thank you.

AWARD WINNING, BESTSELLING AUTHOR

Kathi Barton, a winner of the Pinnacle Book Achievement award as well as a best-selling author on Amazon and All Romance books, lives in Nashport, Ohio, with her husband, Paul. When not creating new worlds and romance, Kathi and her husband enjoy camping and going to auctions. She can also be seen at county fairs with her husband, who is an artist and potter.

Her muse, a cross between Jimmy Stewart and Hugh Jackman, brings her stories to life for her readers in a way that has them coming back time and again for more. Her favorite genre is paranormal romance, with a great deal of spice. You can visit Kathi on line and drop her an email if you'd like. She loves hearing from her fans. aaronskiss@gmail.com.

Follow Kathi on her blog: http://kathisbartonauthor.blogspot.com/

www.ingramcontent.com/pod-product-compliance
Lightning Source LLC
Chambersburg PA
CBHW020621180626
46810CB00007B/2883